Praise for *McKenzie's Friend*

"Dublin-born Davison has created a character in the grand tradition of Sherlock Holmes, Hercule Poirot and Columbo."
—*Irish Echo*

"Philip Davison has a laconic writing style and mordant tone that suits his eccentric protagonist and suits the action, which is quick and nasty."
—*The Baltimore Sun*

"A subtle undercurrent of humour . . . well written . . . weird." —*Time Out* (London)

"Davison shares Beckett's knack for making the down-at-the-heel appear surreal."
—*Times Literary Supplement*

PHILIP DAVISON

McKenzie's Friend

PENGUIN BOOKS

PENGUIN BOOKS

Published by the Penguin Group

Penguin Putnam Inc., 375 Hudson Street,
New York, New York 10014, U.S.A.
Penguin Books Ltd, 80 Strand, London WC2R 0RL, England
Penguin Books Australia Ltd, 250 Camberwell Road,
Camberwell, Victoria 3124, Australia
Penguin Books Canada Ltd, 10 Alcorn Avenue,
Toronto, Ontario, Canada M4V 3B2
Penguin Books India (P) Ltd, 11 Community Centre,
Panchsheel Park, New Delhi – 110 017, India
Penguin Books (N.Z.) Ltd, Cnr Rosedale and Airborne Roads,
Albany, Auckland, New Zealand
Penguin Books (South Africa) (Pty) Ltd, 24 Sturdee Avenue,
Rosebank, Johannesburg 2196, South Africa

Penguin Books Ltd, Registered Offices: Harmondsworth, Middlesex, England

First published in Great Britain by Jonathan Cape 2000
First published in Penguin Books 2003

10   9   8   7   6   5   4   3   2   1

PUBLISHER'S NOTE
This is a work of fiction. Names, characters, places, and incidents either
are the product of the author's imagination or are used fictitiously, and any
resemblance to actual persons, living or dead, business establishments,
events, or locales is entirely coincidental.

LIBRARY OF CONGRESS CATALOGING IN PUBLICATION DATA
Davison, Philip, 1957–
McKenzie's friend / Philip Davison.
p.   cm
ISBN 0 14 20.0198 8
1. Intelligence officers—Fiction.   2. Police corruption—Fiction.
3. London (England)—Fiction.   I. Title.
PR6054.A896 M39 2003
823'.914—dc21   20022034608

Printed in the United States of America
Set in Bembo

For Howard and Shane

With special thanks to my editor, Robin Robertson, for his encouragement and for lending his unblinking eye.

McKENZIE MAN [McKENZIE FRIEND, McKENZIE'S FRIEND] A person who sits beside an unrepresented litigant in court and assists him by prompting, taking notes, and quietly giving advice.

A Dictionary of Law,
Oxford University Press

Oh, all the comrades e'er I had,
They're sorry for my going away,
And all the sweethearts e'er I had,
They'd wish me one more day to stay,
But since it falls unto my lot,
That I should rise and you should not,
I gently rise and softly call,
Good night and joy be with you all . . .

'The Parting Glass', traditional song

Part One

CHAPTER 1

I was on my way to nowhere in particular. I was forty-nine per cent asleep, but watching for a sign in the face of a stranger. I had convinced myself that nothing is ever finished. Somebody who is no longer with us assured me it was so. The forty-nine per cent, I decided, had shut down like an ailing machine. It was some kind of safety feature.

For two days the city had smelt of gas, but I was glad to be out of the flat. Glad to hear the sound of my own feet. Unfortunately, I must have been paying too much attention to my feet because I didn't see the car turn the corner as I stepped off the pavement. It wasn't moving fast, but neither was I. It was a glancing blow that sent me spinning. I hit the ground, stood up immediately, then sat down again on the kerb. The driver flung open his door and came to my aid.

'Are you all right?' he kept asking. He was an old man. His words stretched. They came out of his mouth at half speed.

I assured him that I was all right.

People gathered at the scene. Somebody used a mobile telephone to call an ambulance. Nothing had been broken. So far as I could tell nothing inside me had been damaged. I sat perfectly still for a few minutes, repeating that I was all right. Then, I got up and walked away. I didn't want an ambulance, or the police. The pain in my thigh where I had made contact with the car began to grow, but was no impairment. I would have a large bruise, that was all. My pace quickened. I broke into a run.

I was fully awake again, but now I needed somewhere in particular to go.

This was my adopted city. It was not London, where I belonged. I was not sentimental about London. London wasn't safe for me, so I tried to be practical. I tried not to think about the place. My father still lived in London. He painted sentimental scenes for Christmas cards in his attic. He did this work with great precision. There is nothing sentimental about my father. Now that he's old he meets his friends to swap pills doctors have prescribed for their respective illnesses. This is also done with exactitude. They trade their medications to make the pain of old age perfect. It lets them slither out of the cold embrace of despair. The past is a dangerous domain. They know it and that is how they come to draw strength from the stories they tell one another as they swap their pills. There is nothing sentimental about my father's stories. When he speaks to me he uses a voice that suggests he has been thinking about what he has to say for half a lifetime. Perhaps that is why I nod my head solemnly, though I'm sure he is repeating himself. He writes a good letter. Writes it in that formal, civil service style with its clicks and loops. He speaks like that on the telephone. 'We know how others will end up,' he'd told me last time I'd called, 'but not ourselves.' Then, for some reason, he felt he had to entertain me by painting a picture for me in the ether. This was out of character. Something must have upset him. He described how he had taken a fly-rod up on to the roof of a fishing-tackle shop to test it. Had we been together in the same room he would have given me a feeble demonstration. This is a man who is obsessed with artists and villains. He knows all about the wars of Africa, past and present. I know if I mention corruption I will see his face come alive. I will see him draw strength as he fills his lungs to speak on the matter.

Now that I was fully awake, it occurred to me, I might never again be able to sleep. That night I sat in the chair by the open window. I thought about dead people, duped people, people walking around department stores smelling of sour clay. Smelling of gas.

I nursed my sore leg. At four o'clock in the morning I saw three men advancing down the middle of the street. They wore reflective vests. There was a distinctive rhythm to their movements. There was an efficiency and a harmony to their progress. They were water men. They deployed their listening rods as part of their dance. Was somebody making a pop video?

The road was going to be dug up again. There was one spot in particular towards which they were rapidly advancing. It was just before the junction. They had dug up this piece of road repeatedly. From my window I watched the water men follow the route of the mains pipe under the street. They moved swiftly until they came to the jinxed spot, where they detected trouble. Each man in turn put the wooden cup of his rod to his ear and listened intently.

'Yes, that's it,' I said aloud. 'Right there.'

They moved the points of their rods just a foot at a time now.

'Can't you see the patches?' I mumbled. 'Isn't it obvious? There's something down there nobody can fix.'

When your world has shrunk you're apt to be short-tempered.

I wanted to listen to the flow myself; to hold a rod; to move as they moved. I strained to hear their brief exchanges but could not make out their words at this distance.

Perhaps if I went down and talked to them – told them that the occupants of our house had experienced no difficulty with the water supply: no discolouration; no drop in pressure, except, of course, when the supply was shut off so the work could be done. They would know what was being done about the smell of gas.

I went to the kitchen sink and splashed my face with water. I had to get out more often, I decided. Harry Fielding wasn't going to be knocked down again.

If rolling clouds make any sound then what I heard when I returned to the window was the sound of clouds rolling. Some time before dawn I crawled back into bed and fell asleep instantly. When I woke it was a hot morning but my eyeballs were cold in their sockets. I lay there thinking I could hear the water drain into the bottom of the plant pots. Thinking I could hear an elephant trumpeting in the zoo, the sound carrying across the noise of the city. I closed my eyes and I heard the voices in the pub on the corner of the street. The pub was full of journalists and policemen. Shutting my eyes tighter still I could see the snow of the previous winter – china cups falling out of the sky and landing without a sound. I speak many languages, only one of which I understand.

A breeze opened the flap of a manila envelope on the table. There was a dead sparrow in it. The bird had got into the room in my absence and hadn't been able to get out. I was looking at the envelope, trying to decide what I to do with it, when the shadow of a construction crane crossed the floor and made me jump. Recently, my father had been seeing extraordinary shapes in the clouds. Now, I was jumping over shadows.

I was used to being on my own. Used to days that had little or no shape; days that unwound in somebody else's pocket. But now, I was restless. My neighbour, Uberto, from Naples, came and went at odd hours. Often, he carried a grip bag. He would set off with grim determination, as if he were going to murder somebody. Suddenly, I had a strong urge to follow him.

My body had ached even before the accident. I had been swimming in a river of sticks. I bent down and touched my toes. Exercise in the morning prolongs your life, according to my promiscuous aunt. But this is from a woman who has strange yellow feet, and eyebrows in the wrong place. She tells me she has outlived all her lovers because of her exercising. Credit her with some small, forgotten kindness and she is immediately suspicious. Her sort always lives a long life.

I was contemplating Aunt Kate's resilience when I straightened my tarpaper suit and stepped into my shoes.

I lifted the telephone and rang my father. I invited him to come on a fishing trip with me. I described the route and the terrain. He was surprised at my interest in fishing. He was right to be suspicious. I wasn't well, I had decided. I needed therapy. I had a picture of myself in a rowing boat drifting in the middle of a lake.

I could hear him thinking over the proposition.

We were like taxi driver and carriage-office official staring into the middle distance at a mental map, one attempting to chart the route for the other. It was a severe test.

Yes. He would come, he told me. I knew that I should not be thrown by his apparent lack of enthusiasm. This was a man for whom every journey, however short, was sacred. I could see him standing by the telephone, his big, heavy head hanging off his neck. His sour face peeling off his skull. The whole, heavy head hanging there above the ground like half a bollocks, as he pondered whether or not he had made the right decision.

I watched the crane operator climb up to his cabin, one big hand reaching slowly above the other. A sloth on amphetamine. Sure-footed whether stoned or drunk.

'There was a call for you, Harold,' he said.

That put an end to my redemptionist visions.

'Who called?' I asked.

'He said his name was Alfred.'

'Alfie,' I said, quickly correcting him. 'He said his name was Alfie.'

Reluctantly, my father agreed that the caller had used the informal version of his given name.

8

'What did he want?'

'He didn't say.'

'You didn't ask?'

'I didn't ask and he didn't say,' my father replied. There was a great measure of vanity in his scorn.

An alarm bell had begun to ring in my head. Its ringing carried across the same distance as the trumpeting elephant, but this sound made me shudder.

'He said nothing? He just asked to speak to me?'

'Oh, he knew you wouldn't be here. He said he had lost your number and needed to contact you urgently.'

I knew not to ask if he had given Alfie my number.

'I didn't give him your number,' he said pointedly. His precise anticipation of my fears was uncanny. I had a sudden urge to unburden myself of all the sound reasons for my fears. If I kept my mouth shut perhaps my sordid little secrets would leak out from under my gums.

'Of course not,' I heard myself say. I parried the suggestion with a little wave of my hand. The shadow of the crane chopped the legs from underneath me.

I pictured my father with his head tilted back, the handset held half an inch from his large, dry ear. He adopted this pose when the food he was chewing was too tough or otherwise not to his satisfaction. He would raise his chin and grind the food in a manner that suggested he had teeth all the way down his throat. It was his way of showing his disapproval.

I reverted to the subject of the fishing trip, but my mind was racing. Alfie was trouble. I confirmed the arrangements. As casually as I could I ended with a firm instruction –

'By the way, if Alfie rings again you tell him you

were speaking to me and that I said no. Whatever it is, Harry says no.'

He knew I didn't want the contact number Alfie had left, but he was determined to discharge his responsibilities to the letter.

'His number is here if you want it. I've written it down.'

I thanked him and declined. I was determined that would be the end of it. A policeman with knowledge of some personal history that was best forgotten could not be part of any therapy.

Forget about Alfie, the little voice said. Don't speculate. Don't worry over what he might want.

Alfie wanted me to do something that was certainly illegal, and probably dangerous, or he wanted me to lie to his colleagues, or to come up with information that would put the screws on somebody else –

I really had to learn to stop speculating.

I took a long look out the window at the crane operator suspended under the swinging boom across the street. They had knocked down a terrace of crumbling shops. There was a new piece of sky. The street was getting more light than it deserved. The sun shone into my room for an extra twenty minutes. The local credit union had paid off the loan sharks who were operating in the adjacent streets. The borrowers were now paying back on terms they could afford. Somebody was sweeping up the pools of auto glass on the pavements from the car break-ins. Things must have been improving in other neighbourhoods, too. I'd seen coconuts drifting down the river.

I was living on a test route for learner drivers. There was a regular procession passing through my street. Some learning, some being tested. The instructors liked to use the near corner for the reversing manoeuvre. I had got into the habit of muttering instructions over the rim of my coffee mug. I had developed my own system of judging accuracy and was keenly sensitive to what they called 'lack of progress'.

As I passed judgement on one creeper, Alfie spoke to me. From a great distance, but with remarkable clarity. Harry, he said, I'm a dead man. You've heard dead men talk, haven't you, Harry? You and I know they do nothing else. The dying mumble. The dead talk. Talk. Talk. Talk.

In spite of the great distance I could smell Alfie's breath. Garlic and peppermint. The garlic and peppermint helped Alfie lie. His hands were like ginger root. With these ginger-root hands he made small, concise gestures. This was his way of demonstrating that he was a reasonable man. Alfie lied with his hands as well as with his mouth.

Alfie had grown up in Gibraltar. He liked people to know that. It helped to set him apart. It encouraged friend and enemy alike to see him as a man with more to prove in order to gain acceptance. He liked to think his outsider status provided a credible basis for his cheek and his abrasive charm. I was never taken in by the charm. I had glimpsed a better man underneath.

It was plain to me that a man with his complexion was never meant to live in a Mediterranean climate. He told me he had gone to school on a ship that was moored in the harbour. Perhaps that explained how he had come to make his voice clearly audible over such a distance.

To hell with Alfie. The driver being tested was going to pass. The crane operator was not going to make a slip, whether stoned or drunk. I was going fishing with the old man somewhere under that new piece of sky.

I made coffee. I made toast with two heels of a sliced pan. I hadn't been out to the shops for a week or more so I ate it dry.

I sat in my chair. My eyes wandered about the room until they fixed upon the door. Suddenly, I was anxious about unexpected visitors. I fixed on the doorknob. Whoever had had the room before me had replaced the plain handle that would have matched what was on the other side with a beehive-shaped brass knob. The plain keyhole cover been replaced with a bee pressed in metal. It was an expensive device, pleasing to the hand. I began to wonder why someone would leave behind such an object when they moved. They must have left in a great hurry, I decided.

Many people living alone look at door handles. I was one among that minority. There is a limit to the number of minorities to which you want to belong. I sprang out of the chair and took off out the door, down the stairs and out into the street. My father's solitary existence was on my conscience of late and now I was doing something about it. I had a mission.

I needed to organise transport for the trip. I knew where I could hire a car at a good rate.

I passed an old woman. Her legs were clad in loose surgical stockings. She had stopped to sweep aside a flattened plastic bottle with her foot. I crossed the road on the shadow of the crane boom. I saw the yellow marks on the road where they were going to dig.

On the reverse-manoeuvre corner I came upon a frail old man taking great pleasure in beating his dog with a stick. It seemed to be some kind of exercise. He got to expend his limited energy in public and to use what strength he possessed. The dog took the beating, but grumbled and growled. For the old man this was a bonus.

I put a spring in my step, in spite of a stiff leg. To hell with Alfie, I thought, I'm going fishing.

Solly owns a backstreet garage. He has a large family and a small terrace house without a garden. Each of his children has a job in the garage after school. Solly is respected in the neighbourhood. He doesn't have private space to park the cars in need of repair; he just has his garage workshop. He and his two apprentice mechanics park these cars in the adjacent streets. Each car gets one of Solly's business stickers. None of these cars has ever had a window smashed. Nobody steals from Solly, or from Solly's customers. A visitor's car with its bumper shunted against the bumper of a car bearing one of Solly's stickers is afforded the same protection.

The youngest child has the job of putting the sticker on the back window. It is never quite straight, never quite in the centre, but it seems that all of Solly's customers recognise the honour that is being bestowed with the affixing of the badge. There are never any complaints. The crooked sticker is never re-positioned.

There is also a complimentary valet service. Solly

insists that every customer gets his ashtray emptied and the car gets a free wash with a garden hose and a sweeping brush. There is never a complaint about the streaks; never a complaint about the delay. There is always loose change for the children.

I had been introduced to Solly through a mutual friend. That was enough for Solly to count me worthy of his auto repair and protection scheme.

I also avail myself of his personal car pool arrangement. Neither Solly nor I actually own a car. There is always a car available to Solly and Solly can always make a car available to me. He won't let me hire it, but I give him a very generous tip to be shared out among the army of children who go through the motions of making it ready.

When I came around the corner that morning he emerged from his workshop cleaning his nails with a screwdriver. This was not a leisurely act. He was agitated. He looked down the lane and gritted his teeth.

'Harry,' he said, 'never trust a man who doesn't have a watch.'

I didn't bother asking why he advocated this because I presumed he felt that a man without a watch was a bad timekeeper. This was a mistake.

'You trust a man without a watch?'

I spluttered at the challenge, then I said, no, I did not.

'They're mean bastards. They're tight. Tight as a drum. Tight, mean, smug bastards. What do you want? I haven't time to be talking.'

'I need a car.'

'Everybody needs a car. How long do you want it?'

'Until Tuesday.'

He gave me a hard look.

'All right,' I said, 'Monday evening, then. I can park it and post the keys through your letter-box.'

'You're another tight bastard,' he said. 'You can have it until first thing Friday.'

'Thanks, Solly. You're a pal.'

'There's something just fixed. The owner wants to sell. We'll take it for a test.'

This was not the kind of test I observed from my window. The word 'test' meant something different to Solly. When a car came back from one of Solly's test drives it smelt of chips and vinegar. The windows would be smeared with children's greasy fingerprints.

He had a filthy cushion he threw on the driver's seat as a concession to the customer's upholstery. Solly now gave a shrill, short whistle and a hand signal to one of his apprentices to indicate that he wanted the keys to one particular car. This signal was also taken by the children present as an invitation to scramble into the back seat.

Solly got his filthy cushion.

'Where will we go?' he asked.

His children suggested the airport. As a big treat he took his children to the airport for their tea. This was popular with his wife. The suggestion, however, was completely ignored.

'Will we go up and take a look at the fires?'

He was referring to the gorse fires that had been raging in the mountains for two days. There had been extensive reports in the newspapers about the damage. This was not a question, of course. He had already turned over the starter motor and engaged the gear. We took off down the lane with three of his brats in the back seat, the youngest bawling his eyes out.

It wasn't a mad rally drive up into the mountains. Solly is a very careful driver. He did, however, take us very close to the fires. To him, it was a spectacle. He had no sense of danger about it. The long ribbon of fire and smoke stretched around us in an arc with the city below. Solly explained his theory to his children – some bastard had pitched a bottle into the gorse, the thick end of the bottle had magnified the sunlight and had started the fires. We would have to come back at night, he said, to get the full effect.

Back in the city, Solly pronounced the car to be in good working order and handed me the keys. For the following two days and nights the gorse fires raged in the mountains and the car remained parked across the street from my room. The site foreman didn't like it being there, but made no enquiries about it. The learner drivers gave it a wide berth. Maybe they all knew about Solly's magic stickers.

Early on the third morning I drove it to the airport to collect my father. The dead bird was in the glove compartment. I had meant to ditch it earlier. When I was getting out of the car I finally sealed the envelope and propped it against the wall in the car park. Anybody with the smell of gas in their nostrils finding a dead bird might have thought it had fallen out of the sky. However, they might have been altogether more interested in how it had come to be sealed in a manila envelope.

My father was wearing sporty clothes, and this was

a surprise. He looked much older than I remembered from our last encounter, some eight months earlier, but he also seemed more relaxed. As he came through the arrivals hall he was almost enjoying himself, I thought.

In an earlier life he had surrounded himself with those he called 'scruff' because he felt they looked up to him. These people were opportunists. Good-time Charlies. He had had the same relaxed air then as now.

When we had put his luggage and the rods he had brought for both of us in the boot, he looked at the car and asked how far we had to go in it.

The drive to the lakes was uneventful. He didn't seem much interested in the details of the landscape. It was as if we were travelling the familiar route home.

'There used to be a great oak forest here,' I said as we drove across open farmland, 'until it was chopped down to build ships to conquer the world.'

'Ah-yes, I see,' he said, as though the stumps were still visible.

Then, he said that he was happy to see me. Happy to be taking me on this fishing trip.

I glanced at him and smiled. He was looking away into the distance. I said nothing. I anticipated that there would come a moment when I could tell him that I was happy to see him.

It felt good to be out on the lake. I was contented enough knowing that beyond the trees which lined the shore my father was under the bonnet of the car, bungling his attempt to improve the performance of the engine. The car had spluttered several times on the journey. He was very keen to get out fishing in our hired rowing boat, but he had insisted on attending to the car first.

I pulled in the oars. When the old man was ready I would row to the shore and collect him. Until then I would let the boat drift. Letting the boat drift was a big step for me. I had been looking for something spiritual, something inclusive. I wanted to be part of the sensual world about me, to trample down the past with a primitive sense of awe, however forced.

The water was flat. The sun shone in a blue sky. The trip was already a success. I sat down on the bottom of the boat, put my feet up, crossed my ankles. The boat rotated with a gentle bobbing motion in the middle of the lake. I listened to the bird-calls. The trees on the shore passed slowly behind my boots. I felt the sun on my shoulders and the back of my neck. I speculated as to how most of us passed through our own private darknesses and survived and found a way to heal ourselves. I was thinking about the crane operator, his view of the gorse fires on the mountain. I was envying him his altered state when a figure standing on the lake shore drifted into the 'V' created by my splayed feet.

It was not my father. This man was wearing a dark, tight-fitting suit with a white shirt. He had pink hands and a pink face. He was a sinister marzipan pig in his Sunday best. He motioned to me with a slow, deliberate wave. I shaded my eyes. Initially, I did not react. Initially, I did not recognise him. He was too pink, too hot and bothered, too much out of his element. I let him wave, and I kept my eyes fixed on him.

Then, he struck a familiar confrontational pose and I realised that this sinister marzipan pig was Alfie.

CHAPTER 2

I rowed towards the shore. When I looked over my shoulder to steer my course Alfie's intrusive voice carried effortlessly across the water and bounced off my forehead.

'Harry,' he exclaimed, 'don't you look the picture in a rowing boat.'

I said nothing.

'You're stiff as a poker, Harry. You need a holiday. You should be stretched out, not rowing a boat.'

He had grown an extra mouth just to repeat the insult.

'I'm fine, Alfie,' I said. 'Thank you for your concern.'

'What are you looking into the bushes for?' he asked with a broad grin. 'There's nobody else.'

That broad grin told me he had some awkward questions for me. He was going to ask his questions and cock an ear to listen for lies. Some people have a good pair of eyes. Some people can hear things the rest of us miss. Then, there are a few like Alfie. Their ears have eyes. Alfie would listen to lies with mordant glee. People foolishly mistook this for gullibility.

I looked at his pink, grinning face.

'What's wrong with you?' I asked. 'Shoes too tight?'

Making a show of his getting my goat seemed to be the sensible thing to do.

'You're annoyed because I followed you here, aren't you?' he said. 'Well, I can understand that. I'd be annoyed if you followed me – of course, you wouldn't catch me in a rowing boat. You wouldn't have to fight your way through swamp and thicket to greet your old pal Alfie. Had I known you were coming to a place like this I would have bought insect repellent.'

'You followed my old man?'

'Yes, I followed your old man. Then, I followed you both up here. The Harry I knew would have spotted me. Maybe you don't need a holiday after all. You need work.'

'I have a job. The answer is still no.'

'Harry, will you get out of that boat? You're making me sick watching you go up and down. Why don't you let your old man do his fishing in the boat and you and I go for a drink?'

'No.'

Alfie looked up at the blue sky. 'Rain on the way.'

'I'm not made of sugar.'

'You're making me feel ridiculous, standing here.'

He really didn't want to be out in the heat. For all his skilful tailing, he hadn't come prepared. He had stepped off a London street. Even close up he looked like a sinister marzipan pig.

A deceptive, lazy whistle came from the far shore. My father stood patiently in a foot of water holding two fishing rods.

'Look,' said Alfie, 'your father wants his fish.'

I'm sure Alfie saw my eyes grow dull in their sockets.

'Just one drink, Harry,' he said.

Flies were buzzing around Alfie's head. He swiped at them with his hand. He was still grinning.

I rolled down my sleeves.

Alfie's grin broadened with relief.

'There's nothing to worry about,' he said.

How many lies could I detect in that short statement?

You don't have to think when you are out fishing. Isn't that the point? You can get lucky and catch a fish. You can get pleasantly drunk. Eventually, of course, you start thinking. When you are having a good time you are apt to think that you are brighter than you thought, a more able survivor, a better judge of character. That can be dangerous. You say yes when you should say no.

Alfie raised his hand and gave one of his slow waves and called to my father by his first name, which he had got from the telephone directory.

'Cecil! Cecil, come and join us. We're going for a drink.'

My father stood his ground for a moment, then turned away.

When I saw Alfie take his first drink I could see that it was medicine. The second drink drained the cockiness out of him. I knew then that he was in trouble.

'Nice spot here,' he said.

Alfie liked to probe for any vulnerability. He was expert at probing. He liked to poke at a person's sensibilities. Just before his poking drew the disdain he justly deserved, Alfie would retract completely and display a generosity of spirit that said – I'm really not that hard, not that cruel. This was Alfie's way of ingratiating himself. 'Nice spot here' didn't ring right at all.

'Isn't it,' I replied.

'Your old man drag you up here?' he asked.

'How did you know?' I asked.

'I can tell,' he said. 'It doesn't suit you. You look like a right fool in a boat. I watched you row.'

'You did? Well then, you might have learnt something.'

'I've always liked you, Harry,' he said. He managed another of his grins, though this one did not last.

'Alfie, I'm busy.'

'Of course you're busy. I can see that.'

'I have a life.'

'You have a job?'

'Yes. I have a job.'

'I bet you curse your old man for dragging you way up here. You're too busy to go fishing, but you can't say no. You have to indulge him. He's old. What job do you have, Harry?'

That was when he had his second drink.

'You're not listening,' I said.

'I'm listening.'

'Whatever it is, the answer is no.'

'I'm listening. I hear you.'

He was attentive, but it was not reassuring. He was like a chimpanzee listening to a watch.

'Nothing is simple any more,' he said. 'You can't just do your job.'

This was rich coming from a man who always knew

the price but never could judge the value. A man with a police badge and a pocket full of sweet wrappers; Alfie, my friend, who regularly took backhanders.

'Why do you look at me like that?' he asked, and ordered another short.

I told him to ease up on his drinking. I hadn't given up my afternoon to listen to a friend with a soft head. He ordered coffee. He was given a cup of instant with two plain biscuits on the saucer.

He didn't speak for some time. Alfie had a habit of stroking his nose, and when he stroked his nose he seemed a little perplexed. It was as though he could not quite believe how much it had grown in the night. He was doing it now.

You've got me wrong, I wanted to say. You wouldn't want me standing next to you in a burning building.

I said nothing. I could see his patience was hammered out of rage, so I sat well back and I watched him. Eventually, he began to talk.

He told me he had been suspended from the police force pending an inquiry. He had been caught taking money from club managers and skin traders. The chief constable was going to make an example of him.

'This extra work,' I said, 'it was something you inherited? It came with the beat?'

'Yes.'

'You couldn't say no. It came with the job.'

'Yes.'

'Yes. And there were others to consider. You didn't want to embarrass your colleagues – what would they do with your share? . . . You found yourself on the spot.'

He was enjoying our candid exchange. Anything that could be construed as a righteous tone fuelled his sense of purpose.

'A tax on dirty money . . . ?'

'Some good comes of it. That's a fact.'

'*And* you don't have to ask for it, right?'

'Right.'

'They just give it to you. What else do you get? Free drinks? Last month's skin magazines? Dinner from the set menu?'

'Most of them aren't that generous, Harry.'

Alfie had a reputation for charming every class of thug and pocket gangster. Legend had it that he was respected among criminals as a hard man dedicated to a private *laissez-faire* system. A family man who believed in vigorous free enterprise as a guarantee of his children's future success.

In fact, he had no children.

He was known for his particular strain of honesty – 'Be careful what you say,' he would caution his inform-ers. 'Anything you tell me goes back to the chief. It goes straight on to the file.' This was to encourage a more responsible informant, he would insist.

The whole policing system was growing ever more reliant on informants, and, increasingly, informants were the possessions of individual policemen. Alfie encouraged his choirboys, as he called them, to act as though they were the law. Then, he would slap them down just when they expected his praise. That made him a hard master to please.

His high expectations flattered most who served him. When they sang to him they found it difficult to hold back anything. All of Alfie's choirboys wanted to please him.

He liked to introduce himself to villains. He would seek them out in the clubs, bars, car parks and restaurants, and shake them by the hand. He would give them one of his grins. He would then list his accusations. He would write in his greasy notebook as, inevitably, each accusation was dismissed – 'Denied,' he would mumble as he scribbled.

I expect he had learnt this from the tabloid journalists he liked to count among his friends. These people never seemed to notice that he treated them just as he treated the villains. There was the same systematic airing of accusations; the same grin. The caution issued to his informants was also issued to his journalist friends. Alfie told me he was endlessly enthralled by the one-man investigative documentaries on television. These were rivalled only by the nature programmes, he said.

When he had eaten the two biscuits, he began his story.

'I'm standing under a railway bridge,' he said, launching into it abruptly. 'I'm watching soup being doled out of a van across the street. I'm on the lookout for one of my choirboys. They call him Boxer – he has a reputation for fighting other people's battles. Any provocation at all and he comes out fighting. Very able with his hands and his feet. Boxer had some information for me, but he was avoiding me. I was watching that soup queue because I couldn't find him in the usual places and I'd seen him there once before. That last time he had called me over with a crooked finger and I'd had a talk with him in a doorway. So, Harry,

I'm standing under the bridge and suddenly my head begins to spin and my guts begin to burn. Suddenly I'm lying on my back looking up at the underside of a train that's pounding over me. The noise is terrible. This is the train from hell and I'm on fire. Someone had poisoned me, Harry.'

'You took something?' I asked.

'No, I didn't take anything,' he barked. 'The pub I'd just been in – somebody in there had slipped something in my drink. I know because they'd sent this little tomboy to watch me and report. I saw her across the street watching me squirm on the pavement. She was standing with the old men. The old men were just looking at me over the rims of their soup cups. My arms and my legs went numb. When I started retching this tomboy came closer. She had a sweet, innocent face but she had that what-do-you-call-it – eczema. Harry, she was determined to turn in a detailed report . . .'

He left a long silence. He was not looking for sympathy. He was attempting to strip his story down to facts.

'Anyway,' he said, suddenly looking at me directly, 'as you can see, I survived.'

I could see a corrupt copper exposed. A complicated man crudely knocked on his back.

In many respects Alfie was an excellent police detective, but now he was suspended. The people he had been taking from had taught him a lesson. There must have been quite a few who would gladly have seen him crippled or dead.

'You know who did it?' I asked.

'No.'

'You know what they put in your drink?'

'They told me at the hospital. They said I was lucky it was a small dose. They said I was lucky I wasn't blind.'

'And you're telling me I'm the one who needs a holiday.'

He grunted.

'You're a bent copper, Alfie. You should be more careful.'

He leant back to study me. Then, he grinned.

'I knew you would see it for what it is,' he said. 'We're here to celebrate my good fortune.'

I remembered he had once told me that loyalty was the difference between 'the right thing and the other thing'.

He still hadn't told me what he wanted from me. I thought that if I told him I didn't want to leave the old man out on the lake by himself it would prompt some kind of request or demand.

None was forthcoming.

I left him there to drink, with a promise to return with my reluctant father to celebrate Alfie's deliverance. I went back to the lake.

My father was sitting motionless in the rowing boat on the flat water. He looked like one of the water-colour figures he painted on his cards in the attic. The line on his rod was taut and he was hunched over, gazing at the point where it entered the water. He had been so surprised by my invitation that he had forgotten the wax for his line.

I whistled.

He reeled in with great care. What was he afraid

of? – that he would find his line attached to a plug and see the lake drain before his eyes?

He rowed slowly to the shore.

'Well,' he said dryly. 'Animal, vegetable or mineral?'

'Alfie's a friend,' I said, 'that's all.'

I could see he was watching me for a signal.

'We don't want him here, do we?'

'There's nothing wrong with him,' I said. 'There's nothing to worry about. He's just an old friend. You don't know him,' I added stupidly.

He nodded.

'We can afford a little time to be sociable, can't we?' I said.

'Sociable?'

'He's a police detective.'

'And he wants to socialise?'

'I told him we'd have a drink with him.'

'You told him you would be here?'

'Yes,' I lied. 'He said he might be in the neighbourhood. You catch anything yet?'

'Yes. A pike. And I threw it back.' This was a deliberate and conspicuous little lie. It was his way of challenging my hollow assertions.

'Well, are you coming?'

He looked at me, then he effortlessly stood up in the boat. 'Of course I'll have a drink with you, Harold.'

When we got back to the pub we found that Alfie had created a scene. He had repeatedly made a pass at a young local woman. He had invited trouble with what he later described to me as harmless flirting. There was tension in the air. He had been threatened by several of the men present and these were not men given to idle threats.

'Sit down there, Harry,' Alfie bellowed. 'Have a drink. Cecil, sit down with us. Let me introduce you to my new little friend . . .' He swung around unsteadily, looking for the woman.

One man got off his stool and came to the front, his fists clenched. He leant into Alfie's face.

'Get out,' he said in a low, even voice.

Alfie did not flinch.

'That's enough, Alfie,' I said. 'Put on your jacket. We're leaving.'

While Alfie struggled to put on his jacket I looked for my father in the dark corner where he had been standing, but he had slipped away. I pushed Alfie towards the door. He was grinning again. I wanted to slap his face, but that would have drawn the pack down on him. I was not going to say any more. I just wanted him out of there in one piece.

'Good night,' Alfie announced.

I squeezed his arm to let him know that he should keep his mouth shut. Everybody just stared.

'Carry on,' Alfie bellowed.

I squeezed harder.

'I thought these people were meant to be friendly,' he muttered loudly to me.

I pushed him out through the door. My father was sitting in the car across the car park with the engine running.

'Cecil!' Alfie cried, and waved awkwardly.

'I'm all right,' he said to me and pulled away from my

grip. Like all drunks, he was trying to behave soberly. He walked towards the car like a man on stilts.

Three men came out of the pub, calling after him. They had been standing at the back wall and had taken no part in the confrontation. 'Hey, mister,' one shouted, 'wait a minute. Hold up, there . . .' His was a conciliatory tone. 'Wait. Look, we're sorry. You have the wrong impression . . .'

They wanted Alfie to come back inside. They were embarrassed that a stranger should be spurned over a trivial misunderstanding.

'You'll come back in now and you'll have a drink with us,' another insisted. They were trying very hard to be hospitable.

'I'm sorry,' said Alfie. 'I've made a fool of myself. I've offended that young woman.'

Nonsense, they insisted. They were sorry he had been made to feel unwelcome. One of them took Alfie by the arm. It was altogether a more gentle grip than the one I had applied. He turned Alfie back towards the door, which somebody was now holding open.

'Well, if you insist,' I heard Alfie say.

'We haven't time,' I said, looking him directly in the eye. 'We really should be going. Thanks anyway.'

'You go on,' he said, 'I'll catch up.'

'No,' I insisted, 'we've enjoyed ourselves and now we must leave.' I took hold of Alfie's free arm.

'Just the one,' somebody said, 'we owe him that. You can join us.'

In spite of my grip they began to guide him towards the door. I let go of Alfie and put my hand on the arm of the most insistent Samaritan. I had no doubt that he was the most dangerous. I engaged his eyes directly. I spoke quietly, my pitch matching theirs.

'He may be stupid,' I said, 'but he's with me.'

I clamped Alfie's arm once again and I marched him to the car. The three Samaritans watched. There were others now standing in the doorway of the pub.

'I'm perfectly able . . .'

'Shut up,' I snarled. 'Don't look back. Get in the car.'

Cecil had two passenger doors open. We got in quickly.

'I thought you liked it here,' said Alfie. 'I thought you liked these people. It was just a misunderstanding . . .'

'You fool. Didn't you see what was happening? They were going to take you back in there and beat you to a pulp. Didn't you see that? I'm surprised at you, Alfie. I really am.'

There was a brief silence. If Alfie was feeling sorry for himself it didn't show.

'Cecil, what do you think?' he mumbled, as we sped away.

My father did not reply. Instead, he glanced at me.

'This car is a bad starter,' he said. 'It's unreliable. You should get rid of it.'

CHAPTER 3

'Alfie, you're drunk,' I rasped, 'and that isn't like you.'

He feigned surprise. He pulled an exaggerated face, an expression that suggested somebody had just stabbed him with a barber's pole.

'Anything you have to say about me say behind my back,' he mumbled. He was very pleased with himself for having come up with that.

The remark had a distinct effect on Cecil. He was driving with a clear sense of purpose. Now, he put his foot down on the accelerator. I could not think how he had already decided upon a specific destination. Was he driving back to the city or was he going to pitch Alfie into the lake?

Somewhere I had drawn a faint line beyond which I was determined I would not go, a line that could so easily be missed, a line I could never hope to see at this speed.

'Where do you want to be dropped off?' I blurted out. 'You didn't say where you left your car.'

'Alfred can't drive anywhere in that state, can you, Alfred?' my father said.

'Cecil. You're right. These roads are too dangerous.'

'You'll come fishing with us,' said Cecil. 'You do fish, don't you?'

'Of course I fish,' Alfie replied, curling his lower lip.

'You can use Harold's rod. Harold doesn't care for fishing. You don't mind, Harold, do you?'

Initially, I was shocked at the old man's invitation, but then I saw what was coming. My father had heard none of Alfie's story. He knew nothing of his history, but when the old man looked at Alfie he saw scruff. It was as clear to him as the shapes in the clouds. Not the good-time Charlie kind of scruff. Something altogether more devious and enduring. My father's nose for corruption had been alerted. He was up on his hobby-horse and he was going to take Alfie to task on the subject. A police detective who was prepared to drive while drunk had other things to hide.

In spite of Alfie's fears for his safety on the roads there was no doubt at all that he would have driven had he taken his car to the pub.

'You can continue your touring this evening,' Cecil said. 'There is such a stretch in the evenings. You are touring, I take it?'

'Touring. Yes . . .'

'Beautiful countryside, but dangerous roads.'

Alfie turned his troubled eyes up to the sky. 'And such weather . . .' he said.

Some of the poison was still in him. Its undetectable residue permeated his brain. He carried its chemical print in his nerve ends. Alcohol was not the purifier he sought, but it dulled the voices of dead men, all of whom were talking about Alfie's brush with death. I felt sorry for him. My mistake.

It was absurd – the three of us in a small rowing boat.

I had come to the lake to re-establish a connection with my father; to get the same kick Solly got out of the gorse fires on the mountainside. I had come to marvel at the near impossibility of our existence, and, on a more mundane level, to celebrate my own deliverance. Pulling on a set of oars between these two men served only to make me aware of restrictions.

Alfie was sprawled in the bow, his ginger-root hands clasped behind his head, his lips pressed firmly shut. He no longer resembled a pink marzipan pig. In fact, he appeared quite pale. Cecil was sitting in the stern. He seemed more frail now that we were out in the boat. His sad, worldly expression appealed to Alfie. Alfie failed to see that this was the product of an all-embracing rage that had gone cold over many years.

'You don't look well,' Cecil crowed. 'What's the matter? Are you going to be sick?'

'I'm all right, thank you, Cecil.'

Evidently, Alfie did not see that Cecil's crowing and his sad, worldly expression were at odds with each other.

'Green around the gills.'

'I'm not used to so much fresh air.'

My father grunted and gave a derisive wave of the hand. 'I can give you something,' he said. 'I have something in my bag.'

Christ. He was offering our damaged Alfred some old crony's pills.

'No, thank you, Cecil. I'll be fine.'

'I've something to wash it down with.'

'No . . . really.'

Alfie was oblivious to the possibility of a second poisoning.

'It's for the stomach. I've nothing to counter the effects of alcohol.'

'He doesn't want anything,' I said.

'A man in his position should be more careful what he consumes.'

'You're right,' said Alfie.

Had I not known better, I would have been convinced they were playing games with me.

'A lot of pressure in your line of work,' Cecil observed caustically. 'A lot of stress. Is that it?'

'Yes . . . And you,' Alfie countered, 'you've led an interesting life. I can tell.'

'Interesting. No.'

'You know about people. You can't fool me.' The fresh air had done nothing to reduce the effects of alcohol.

'No.'

'You were a civil servant. Am I right?'

My father did not reply.

'Very interesting,' said Alfie.

'You're in no fit state to fish,' I said.

'You've got me wrong, Harry,' he replied. 'I like to fish – all weathers. Not like you.' Then he grinned. 'You haven't time to fish. You've got the patience, but you just don't have the time.'

He craned his neck to look over my shoulder. 'Your son leads an interesting life, isn't that the truth, Cecil?'

'Around the edges,' my father replied without hesitation.

I had to laugh.

Alfie was familiar with the term 'understrapper'. The Harry Fielding Alfie knew was an understrapper; a bob-a-job man for MI5. Somebody who could do a bit of house- or office-breaking, or some surveillance work. Someone capable of conducting a blackmail campaign for the Whitehall spooks – all done at a safe distance, of course, and none of the targets exotic. Contract work without the contract.

In Alfie's book there was a category of job which he called imaginary. Understrapper was one such imaginary job. He disapproved of cut-price villains and casual muck-shovellers. He dismissed them as misfits; crude operators to a man. He could never appreciate that their gullibility and their expendability were often essential factors.

He saw me as an exception. He thought I had been blessed with a smearing of Whitehall grease. He knew that I had killed a man in Chinatown. He did not know that it had nothing to do with my being an understrapper. He knew I had a Whitehall protector, someone with a grease pot. He did not know who. I had shot a man for beating a woman who had almost been my friend. Had Alfie known this crude fact my reputation would surely have suffered a severe dent.

My father knew less than Alfie about my imaginary job. He knew I had worked for MI5. He imagined something had gone spectacularly wrong, that I had failed in some sordid task and was condemned to a temporary state of limbo.

Around the edges . . . I laughed, but I had a heavy heart. I needed a pair of wings in place of a pair of oars.

I tried to think of something else. I lifted the oars out of the water for a moment, but kept them spread. I let the boat drift. It was early evening. The sun was now low in the sky. The trees on the shore were bathed in a warm light that made each perfectly distinct. I searched the shore for signs of life. Did the city still smell of gas? Were the fires still burning in the mountains? Had the crane operator fallen from his perch in spite of his sure-footedness? Aunt Kate – I should have visited her instead of calling the old man.

'I have two apples in that bag,' my father said. He was offering an apple, not one of his home prescriptions.

'An apple,' said Alfie, 'yes. Thank you. I'll eat an apple.'

Cecil rooted out the two apples. He insisted I have the second one. He waited until Alfie bit into his apple before beginning his interrogation in earnest.

'You do this often?'

'What?'

Cecil left a brief silence. 'Tour.'

'I don't have much time.'

'The life of a policeman, yes . . . Family?'

Alfie didn't like this line of questioning. 'I'm married,' he replied.

'Children?'

'No . . . This is a good apple.'

'I am sorry. You've come here to talk to Harold, not have me ask questions.'

'I'm touring.'

'Of course.'

'Harold told me he would be up here.'

'Did he? I see. And you're touring by yourself.'

'It's a joy to be out here . . . moments like these . . . What do *you* think, Harry?'

'Some people are happy in a new pair of socks.'

'It's a more complicated world than it used to be,' Alfie proposed.

'You think so?' Cecil asked solemnly. 'I don't agree.'

'I don't get much of a chance to do this sort of thing,' Alfie said.

'Too much time spent in court?' Cecil suggested. 'Too much paperwork. You must get quite a headache.'

No. Alfie didn't get that kind of headache. The villain's motto, as he never tired of reciting for those he caught, was – 'If at first you don't succeed, you didn't prepare and you're an idiot.' This dubious gem never went down well and Alfie derived satisfaction from the hostile reaction every time.

Alfie was twenty per cent crank.

'I get to play in a seven-a-side at Heathrow once in a while,' he said. 'Always a tough game. Score a goal in that game and you'll remember it for the rest of your life.'

My father had started fishing. I hadn't realised that he had had his rod and line ready. I said nothing. I pulled in the oars. I ate my apple.

'Are you going to use that rod?' he asked Alfie.

'Oh yes,' Alfie insisted, but made no move.

'You know what you're doing, do you?' Cecil asked.

'I can play football and I can fish,' said Alfie.

'I've always thought Harold would have made a good policeman. I've said that to you, haven't I, Harold?'

'Oh, shut up,' I grumbled.

'Too many people policing our cities are not up to the job. Putting incompetent people in the job – that's a kind of corruption, wouldn't you agree?'

Neither of us replied. Alfie made a point of throwing

his apple core into the water. He aimed to sink it as near to Cecil's line as possible. Then, he leant towards me.

'I need you to come to London,' he said in a low voice.

I shook my head – a slight side-to-side movement.

'Cecil,' I called over my shoulder, 'I don't know what you're thinking putting a rod in his hands. He'll have somebody's eye out.'

Alfie kept his eyes fixed on me. They were watery. His head seemed to be nodding. These were the slight, involuntary movements of a tethered balloon. I could not at that moment determine whether his stare was pleading or threatening.

I made a point of eating my apple core.

I didn't know a person could appear to be grinning while they were throwing up. Alfie gave a convincing demonstration of this a short time after swallowing the last of his apple. He heaved up over the side, then apologised repeatedly. He made a good job of covering his fear with a show of embarrassment, but I caught a flash of that fear in his eyes and it had nothing to do with having drunk too much.

I rowed for the shore with long, heaving strokes. In our wake I saw, or imagined I saw, fish rising to feed on the contents of Alfie's stomach. My strokes grew longer still.

'Where are you staying?' Cecil asked. The old man's curtness suggested that he was bitterly disappointed at having to terminate the interrogation at such an early stage and that he was intending to resume at Alfie's sickbed just as soon as a bed could be found.

I crashed the bow of the boat up on to mud and stones at a low point of the bank, sending the three of us lurching in the one direction.

'Harold,' my father said, pushing Alfie out of the boat, 'take him in his car. Get him a bed. He's driving a blue Corsa.' Cecil was out of the boat quickly. Alfie was dizzy. He was standing in the mud with his legs apart. Cecil studied his face at close quarters. 'I take it you remember where you left your car?' he said loudly. 'Give Harold the keys.'

The old man had noticed Alfie following behind us and I had not. We had driven through towns, along open road and narrow country lanes and I hadn't noticed a blue Corsa behind us at any point in the journey. I needed to wake up fast.

Alfie and I stepped ashore. Cecil rowed himself towards his chosen spot with long, slow strokes. Another sacred journey.

'Thanks, Harry,' Alfie said, as we made our way to his hired car. He put a hand on my shoulder. 'I really appreciate this.' We were walking to the car, but his sincere gratitude informed me that we were on our way to London. He was hugely relieved that I was now sharing what had been his own, private illness.

I turned on him. Swung him on his heels and put a threatening finger in front of his nose.

'Alfie, I'm finished with London. I'm a free man.'

'I have a job for us.'

'For us? There's no us. You have some nerve coming here.'

I set up a brisk pace. He kept up with me, but was

unsteady on his feet and unsure of where he had parked the hired car.

'Your old man is quite a character,' he said.

'You think so?'

'I like him.'

'You do.'

He stumbled.

'I feel much better already,' he said.

'I'm glad to hear it. Are you thinking straight? I hope you've regained your senses. I really do.'

'I'm glad you were here to save me today. Say what you like, Harry, but I can trust you with my life. But you've got this wrong. I want to help you.'

I stopped a second time. 'You do?' I slapped his car keys into his hand. 'Drive safely.'

'I can promise you'll see good money,' he said. He sensed he was making progress. I cursed myself. 'There's no risk,' he insisted. 'And it's a job worth doing. I want you to meet someone. When you hear the proposition, if you don't like it, you walk away and nothing more will be said.'

I made no reply.

'I can see where you get your stubbornness,' he said. 'It's good. I like it.'

'You puke in the water, then you talk about my family.'

He pulled on his big nose. 'You have me there,' he said.

I poked him once on the shoulder. 'I'm not interested in any proposition that has you attached. Get back in the sewer. Don't drink in pubs. Be careful what you eat.'

He let go of his nose. That was when I saw the

mordant glee and I began to seethe with rage. Did he think I was lying? Did he really think I was prepared to get involved?

'Let me put you in the picture,' he said.

Now, he was grinning without it showing. Alfie could do that.

CHAPTER 4

Alfie would have you believe he had been given a second liver instead of a heart; that he could do no lasting damage to himself and consequently could not fully comprehend the damage done to others. This was Alfie's own particular brand of innocence, and the eternal source of his maddening grin. It made my desire for a spiritual connection out on the lake seem, by comparison, rank sentimentality. A joyful sound caught in the throat was nothing as compared to Alfie's grin.

I wasn't desperate yet, but I needed an income. I had lied to Alfie about my having a job. He knew it, but thought I was flush and needed to be coaxed. I had the promise of a job. Concierge of a small city hotel. Concierge – that was the term used. It meant live-in assistant manager cum handyman. Had Alfie known this there would have been no dissuading him from the assertion that it was a cover, a compulsory break from work, an enforced holiday with a nuisance job. He was convinced that the Royal Mint was under orders to print extra money for Harry Fielding. There was no telling him that I was an ex-understrapper and that there were few more humble states. There was no pension. No sick pay. Only my father's bartered tonics.

It was likely that Alfie's infatuation was all part of his act. Part of his protective shield.

'He's late,' I said.

'You have something important you need to do?' Alfie asked.

'Let's eat,' I said.

Our linen napkins were stiff enough to be used as trays. We were sitting in an expensive London restaurant waiting for a wealthy publicist-and-sometime-manager Alfie had arranged to meet.

'Eat some bread,' Alfie barked. He pushed the basket towards me. It had been less than twenty-four hours since we'd been out on the lake, but already a partnership had been established, and I didn't like that.

When we had entered the restaurant he had told the maître d' who we were meeting. We were put at the best table. We were not, however, given menus. Apparently, they would only be put on the table when our host sat down with us. I knew how a publicist earned his money. I could guess how a publicist-and-sometime-manager operated. Alfie was anxious about meeting this man. I thought I should take a leaf from Alfie's book and do a bit of poking.

I called to one of the waiters across the room. 'Excuse me. We'll have our menus now, thank you.'

I could see Alfie tighten as the waiter looked to the maître d', who nodded reluctantly. Three menus were put on our table.

'Tell me again, Alfie, what does this man do?'

'If the lion in the zoo dies as a result of choking on the bones of a five-year-old, our man gets the press in. They photograph and interview children visiting the zoo. He gets them to say they are visiting the lioness who is lonely because she no longer has a mate.'

'I see.'

There was a beat. Then, I had to laugh. Alfie laughed, too.

'You want more bread?'

'You sorry you brought me in on this?' I asked.

'Just eat the bread, will you.'

'I'm going to order my lunch.'

'Fine. Don't let me stop you.'

'You'll pay if he doesn't show?'

'He'll come.'

'I don't pay these kind of prices.'

I started to list aloud the items on the menu.

'Harry . . .'

'What . . . ?'

'You don't need to read me the menu.'

I tipped my chair back on two legs until it rested against the oak panelling. I ran my fingers across the damask wall-covering.

'You know it well, do you?' I asked. 'You come here regularly on police pay? I'm impressed.'

He pulled a sour face.

'Oh,' I said, 'I see. Friends of the management?'

'This man likes to eat here. That's why we're here. It's his favourite restaurant.'

'We'd like to see the wine list now, please,' I called to the maître d'. For some reason this had also been withheld pending the arrival of our host. I was about to get a demonstration of what it meant to be friends of the management.

When Sydney Holland entered his favourite restaurant the maître d' came out from behind the reception desk with a pair of slippers and discreetly placed them by our host's chair. When Sydney Holland had removed his shoes and put his feet into the slippers, he greeted Alfie and myself with a weary sigh. The shoes were taken behind the desk, given a buff, then stored. I immediately felt the heat of Mr Holland's gaze. I was being scrupulously measured against expectations. That was something else I didn't like. What had Alfie said about me? How had he misrepresented me, for he had surely done so.

'Mr Fielding,' Holland said, extending a big hand on a short arm. A short arm which, no doubt, had a long reach and a knock-down jab.

I clasped his hand lightly; I let him do the shaking.

He was heavy but not bloated. A man in his sixties, conservatively dressed and closely shaved. A dense mass with mercury in his veins. He wore flat, round glasses. He was the kind of man who had an expensive hat, scarf and pair of leather gloves in his car regardless of the season. I speculated that somewhere on his person he carried a safety pin which he would use as a toothpick.

'Harry . . . Mr Sydney Holland,' said Alfie with his palm out.

I could tell by the way Holland initially ignored Alfie that theirs was a long-standing relationship. A lopsided arrangement that could lean menacingly in either direction.

'Hello, Sydney Holland,' I said. I had taken an instant dislike to the man, but I was intrigued. 'You can call me Harry.'

Holland smiled. The smile brought a bottle of champagne to the table.

'Harry,' Holland repeated.

'Alfie has told me a lot about you,' I said, which was untrue.

'Has he, indeed?' boomed Holland good-humouredly. 'Well then, Harry, we'll count that as a blessing, shall we?' He spoke in a full voice that was easy to imitate.

Alfie was glaring at me for lying out of turn. Alfie and I went back a long way so, under the circumstances, I ignored him. I was still angry with him. For all his pleading, he had refused to give me details of the job. Against my better judgement, I had to take it on trust. I was doing a good deed helping a friend – that was the way he wanted me to look at it.

'I'm hungry,' I declared.

'Well then,' said Holland, 'we must eat.' He must have sent a signal to the waiter who promptly stepped up to our table, though I saw no signal.

Holland did not look at the menu.

'The fish, Donald,' he said to the waiter. 'You'll like the fish,' he said to us.

'No fish,' I said.

'You don't like fish?' Alfie said, jumping in.

'I don't like fish. I don't want fish.'

Holland wasn't in the least bit irked by our edginess. He was settling nicely into his slippers. He was smiling at me directly. Mr Holland had the quick smile of a promoter. A populist flair that was bogus but, nonetheless, inspired confidence. A Swiss professor of clocks.

'No fish,' I repeated.

'What about the prawns?' he enquired.

'Too tough.'

'Too tough?' exclaimed Alfie incredulously.

'In a place like this,' I said, 'I bet the prawns come in leather jackets.'

Holland gave out a big, round laugh, then ordered two fish dishes and lamb cutlets for one.

'You *do* eat meat?' he asked belatedly.

'If it's not tough,' I replied.

Alfie was hopping mad. I had spoilt the cool façade he had erected. Our host, however, was not disappointed.

London was hot and sticky. There was condensation blurring the face of my wrist-watch. The watch had its own micro weather system that promised to seize the works if I remained in a hostile climate for any length of time. Evidently, the heat did not bother Holland. Whatever the weather, Holland saw some gain and was happy to counsel others. I speculated that in this sticky heat he advocated staying indoors and playing the piano, or taking a book of poetry to the park. Sydney Holland knew that most of us desired an uncomplicated life.

I saw him glancing at my clouded watch.

'I'd have the cutlets myself if I wasn't having the fish,' he said.

'No blood,' I told the waiter. 'I want them well done.'

'Hungry, yes?' Holland asked.

He was looking at me lazily now. I had seen that lazy look earlier, on the faces of hi-fi salesmen. Alfie had parked his car some distance from the restaurant. He had walked with purpose to our destination. I had shambled along behind with a slovenly gait. To the group of pale-faced hi-fi salesmen having a lunchtime smoke on the pavement, I was just another wanderer hoping for a chance encounter that would change his life. This was London, after all.

Whatever role Alfie had cast me in, Sydney Holland had me pegged as an opportunist motivated solely by appetite, and that suited me.

'Alfie tells me you're the best at what you do.'

'Does he? Alfie is a friend,' I said with a vinegar smile, 'you should be sceptical.'

'You miss nothing, he tells me.'

'Is there any hot pepper sauce?'

'Hot pepper sauce . . .' Alfie blurted out, 'for your cutlets?' His elbows were digging into the table linen.

'Yes. West Indian hot pepper sauce. Eat your own lunch, Alfie.'

'Hot pepper sauce,' Holland said, and hot pepper sauce appeared.

I didn't like this vetting, or the smugness that was temporarily eclipsed by Alfie's irritation. I didn't like the cosy exclusivity or the puréed parsnips.

'Can we talk about your problem, Sydney?' I asked.

Alfie had given me the bare bones of the job. Holland's daughter, Vanessa Harquin, was missing. She had disappeared more than a month previously. In the initial stages of the police investigation there had been various pieces of circumstantial information from neighbours that had led nowhere. There had been plenty of gossip and speculation. This, too, had yielded nothing useful. There had been several false sightings. The police had made virtually no progress with her mysterious disappearance. Holland, however, believed that his daughter's husband was implicated, and he wanted his every move watched. With a simple, ominous statement it had been impressed upon Alfie that Toby Harquin was capable of anything. Holland knew that with the police investigation stalled his daughter's Missing Person file would remain open but would be re-labelled 'Non-active' if no progress was made. Alfie had told him as much. He had told me that there would be somebody from the Criminal Intelligence Department at Scotland Yard who would go through the material amassed looking for oversights, but nobody expected this to turn up anything.

Holland wanted Alfie to pick up the case privately and to poke as evidently Holland knew he could poke. To independently employ whatever means were necessary to get at the truth. There was plenty of money available for us to do our work. Alfie had repeatedly reminded me of that.

The fact that Alfie was under investigation did not bother Holland one jot. That was business. This was private. Besides, the suspension meant that Alfie could concentrate on finding his daughter.

Holland took a photograph of his daughter from his wallet and placed it before us on the table. An attractive dark-featured woman in her early thirties with a soft, intelligent gaze. Skinny. Athletic. Nothing like her father.

'You'll find her,' Holland said in a tone that eerily lacked any shred of informed judgement.

From the outset, that seemed to me to be a remote possibility, unless the official investigation had misread the situation entirely. Holland gave me a long, hard look that suggested with tremendous effort he could read my thoughts.

'Alfie,' he said, keeping his eyes fixed on me, 'you *will* tell me the truth, however harsh.'

'We will.'

If she had run away, who or what had she run away from? The reason for running dictates the route of the trace; the nature of the search. Was there a likely accomplice; somebody to run to? If she had run was there evidence of preparation? Had she liquidated assets? Brought with her out–of–season clothing? What had she left behind? Had she severed all connections? Vanished at what cost?

I was assured that nothing pointed to her having run away. They were emphatic. There was no 'other man', and the police had thoroughly investigated all her ex-boyfriends.

Yes but, I wanted to say, there are other scenarios. Holland was being very defensive and Alfie wasn't about to challenge him. I thought it best to let Holland have his say without my interrupting.

He turned to Alfie. 'I've had two clairvoyants approach me offering to help.'

'That's not unusual . . .' Alfie replied, creating a space with a gesture of his hand that was meant to stem any flow of detail.

'I sent them away. Is that unusual?'

'Some people . . .' Alfie didn't get to finish his observation.

He turned again to me. 'I sent them away, but I kept their telephone numbers.' He was reporting to us now and his directness was affecting, in spite of his manner.

'I'm told there are people in South America who chew the leaves of the *salvia* plant to help them find somebody they've lost. Should I chew *salvia* leaves?'

That just made me think about my friend on his back under the railway bridge, his arms and his legs numb. All I could do was nod sympathetically, which could have been interpreted as – 'Yes, chew the leaves.'

'I've been walking a lot. I stop and I stare at people's houses.'

'That's understandable,' Alfie said.

He turned again to Alfie, but this time his eyes were more searching. 'There will be no more false sightings . . . not now?'

'We don't know . . .'

He moved his large face closer to Alfie.

'If one day we must give up – how will we know it is time to do that?'

'In time your description of Vanessa will become more vague – "Vanessa is a happy young woman with dark brown hair . . ."'

'This is when we give up?'

'Then, the computer-enhanced image of her they'll use to make up her age will break your heart.'

'We don't give up then, either?'

'No. There is no giving up for you, Sydney.'

I was astonished at Alfie's candidness. I wasn't used to this kind of compassion. My toes were curling in my shoes.

Holland turned again to me. I could observe in him the heartache and the rage at seeing his daughter's finger-marks in a jar of her face cream.

'I've stopped looking at people's houses, Harry.'

'You have . . . ?'

'I have, yes. Alfie knows what I'm talking about.'

'He does . . . ?'

'Alfie . . . you haven't told Harry what we know?'

'I've painted the broad picture.'

Now that phrase inevitably means you've been duped.

Holland put a second photograph down on the table. This one was of Vanessa with her husband, Toby Harquin, and their daughter. A happy holiday snap. This was the first I had heard of the young girl, but I kept my mouth shut on the matter.

'That's him, Harry. That's the man you must . . . question.'

Alfie did not stretch to look. Nor did he pick up the photographs. He had already been briefed. I had immediate confirmation of this. As I picked up the photograph Alfie spoke –

'I have the details,' he said.

Suddenly, I had lost my appetite. Alfie, however, was digging into his lunch. I knew what he meant by 'I have the details'. The statement had a literal meaning – he had committed relevant information to his greasy notebook. He had ingratiated himself with a show of patience and understanding interspersed with a few impertinent questions. His terse words were also an instruction to me not to ask questions. I was to let Holland tell us what he saw fit to tell us.

It was natural for a person to be reluctant to help somebody who was doing better than himself – Alfie had made this observation before we had got out of his car. That was part of his priming me for the meeting with Holland. Alfie used insults as a kind of digestive lubricant. He was quick to remind me, yet again, that it was he who was asking me to do the job, not Holland.

Holland watched Alfie gulp the champagne. I felt I should protect my friend from his close scrutiny. I held out my glass for more.

Holland poured.

'There isn't anything I wouldn't do to get her back,' he said. Did he assume I was that hard or that stupid and would think otherwise? No. The emphasis was on the word *anything*.

But did he mean get her back, dead or alive, or, was he only allowing for the latter?

'I understand,' I said.

'Of course,' Alfie echoed, then added witlessly; 'you leave it to us, Sydney.'

'You like to drink champagne,' Holland said, nodding at my glass. I was making a fair impression on the contents of the bottle myself.

'I'm just being polite.'

'Alfie doesn't like champagne,' he said. 'He drinks it, but he doesn't like it. He's an odd fish.'

Alfie was about to protest, when Holland leant a little further in my direction.

'A lot of individuals come through my door, Harry, and I have a different relationship with each and every one of them. Every one of them is gifted. Every one is an odd fish. Some can't find their way from the dressing room to the stage by themselves, but they are gifted and I respect them all. I want you to know that.'

I did not know why he wanted me to know that, but I nodded intelligently.

Holland wore a display handkerchief in his top pocket. A white rectangle fitted into the pocket 1950s style. I was sure he had splashed it with cologne in case he needed to wipe gravy from his chin. I fancied he had carefully wrapped a diamond in it, a little something that could be presented as payment for goods or services. I imagined him unfolding the stiff linen and spreading it taut with his fat fingers, making the stone wink.

When Alfie held out his glass for another fill Holland was already reaching for the bottle.

Holland paid the bill in cash and gave a generous tip. Now why did I get the impression that this man was not required to pay any bills in this restaurant? Why did I think he was paying out of vanity?

He didn't leave the restaurant with us. Nor were the slippers exchanged for the shoes. As he stood up to see us off I had a vague sense that he was clearing the way for some other encounter, to be paid for à la carte.

Holland's stiff-backed chauffeur acknowledged Alfie with two sandwiched fingers drawn to his peaked cap in salute. Alfie replied with a curt nod. I gave the man a big, friendly wave, just to be awkward.

Alfie walked purposefully to his car. I plodded beside him. He made a tuneless whistling noise. Nothing was said until we were sitting behind the windscreen, then he sighed. I could see he was relieved. His relief suggested we had stepped out of a world where our survival depended on favours granted, favours received; where a misunderstood remark could see us both damned. This was a curious sigh from a man who operated as Alfie did. Perhaps my imagination was running on. Perhaps it was a sigh of indigestion.

'He thinks we're going to find her,' I said.

'We'll find her.'

'Find her alive – he thinks we'll find her alive.'

'We might.'

'Come on, Alfie. You think she walked into a new life?'

'No.'

'You think her husband killed her?'

'Perhaps.'

'He thinks the husband has her in a cellar somewhere. Get real. You're a policeman. What are the chances of that?'

'It's happened.'

He gave the key a quarter-turn in the ignition, squirted the windscreen with the water jets, set the wipers going.

'You shouldn't be taking the man's money,' I said. 'Let the missing person's investigation run its course.'

'It's done that. There's nowhere for them to go. They're waiting for something to turn up.'

'How did you get involved?'

He switched off the wipers. 'I've known Sydney for some time.'

'I gather that.'

'The husband did the press conference, took part in the reconstruction, made a television appeal, went out searching in his own car. I showed Sydney the confidential psychologist's report on him. It suggests he's lying.'

'You showed him the report?'

'He asked to see it.'

'And you showed it to him.'

'Yes.'

'You owe him a favour?'

'I've known Sydney a long time,' he said.

I thought he might turn to look at me directly at this point to shut me up, but he did not.

'You fool, Alfie.'

'The husband – he's lying. We know that.'

'You don't need me for this.'

'I need a partner,' he said. 'Come on. Don't get soft. We have a job we can do.'

'What was this lunch about?'

'He wanted to meet you. He's entitled. He's paying.'

'How long are we going to run with this before we tell him he's never going to see his daughter again?'

'Harry, let me touch your black heart – I'm telling you, there's a chance this woman is still alive. If she is, we will find her.'

'This is police work.'

'Then call me a zealot. If she's dead I'll investigate.'

I was thinking about Holland's son-in-law and the press conference. Some police press conferences convened in missing person cases I knew generated massive media interest, while others attracted little attention, or the attention was short-lived. There was a formidable array of conflicting factors that contributed to this, few of which were fixed. Perceived circum-stances – mysterious, tragic, sinister. The measure of innocence. The potential for what was loosely termed human drama. Other stories breaking. I didn't need to be a policeman to grasp that. Certainly, Sydney

Holland would have had a comprehensive list of those factors and would have recognised every nuance. His daughter's case was one among those neglected. Had Holland any part in steering it thus, I wondered? If that were so, it would indicate clearly that clues from the general public did not figure in his appraisal of the situation.

I didn't know enough about his world to speculate how that kind of manipulation might work. I was still smarting from the demonstration with the slippers.

'You need me to keep you on the dry?' I said.

Alfie made no reply. He started the engine, and pulled out into the road.

'I can see to it you don't trip on the kerb or cause offence.'

There was a long pause, then he momentarily engaged my eyes directly. He spoke with disarming candour –

'Just watch my back, will you?'

His direct plea made me feel ashamed of my harshness, but that shame quickly passed for I was already watching Alfie's back. Secretly, I felt that once again I was connected.

Alfie put a jazz tape in his cassette player. The cassette player seemed to be operated by the accelerator. The mellow trombone music surged when he put his foot down, then went slow and sour when he changed down through the gears. He didn't seem to notice, so I pointed it out.

'Yes, I know,' he said. 'Terrible, isn't it?'

My new-found feeling of magnanimity was soon tested.

'We're not going to listen to it like that, are we?'

'It's good music,' he said. 'It makes me relax.'

Was he profoundly tone-deaf? Could his brain some-how compensate? Were these bizarre surging notes some kind of welcome torture that reasserted a mundane reality?

'It's driving me crazy,' I told him.

'I've been meaning to have somebody look at it, but . . .'

He jabbed his chest with an open hand.

Blame the scum who poisoned his drink – that was the implication.

CHAPTER 5

Earls Court. Leave it to Alfie to find a stinking flat in a nice neighbourhood. It was a basement to which we could have access only via a narrow staircase from the main hall. I forced open the swollen sash window. I took off my jacket. Suddenly, Alfie was concerned, and not about the damp reek.

'You can get a gun?' he said. He made a question sound like a statement.

I turned to face him. 'Gun?'

'A gun?'

'There's no gun, Alfie.'

He didn't like that. It made him grit his teeth.

'Well don't worry about it.'

'I'm not worried about it.'

He stuck two fingers into the soil of a sickly potted plant and pulled out a small bundle wrapped in plastic and secured with a rubber band. From the plastic he took a roll of money. He peeled off a wad.

'Here,' he said. 'Pocket money.'

'You want me on this job or you want somebody with a gun.' Now, *I* was making statements instead of asking questions.

No reply.

'You want a thug who'll shoot the eyes out of somebody for sugaring your tea.'

He was doing a little nervous dance. He pressed the money into my hand.

'There's a phone upstairs, in the hall.'

'What do I need a gun for, Alfie?'

'When a reason presents itself it will be too bloody late, won't it?' he barked, then quickly checked himself. 'Harry . . . please.'

The window was open, but there was no wind, no movement in the air save that generated by a child swinging on a gate two streets away.

'What are you doing in this place? It stinks.'

'Here. Want one of these?'

'No. I don't want a peppermint, and I don't want a gun. A short time ago I was out on a lake fishing. Now, I'm standing in this kip.'

'You don't like fishing.'

'You still married?' I could see nothing in the flat that suggested anything other than a bachelor dive. 'Where's your wife?'

'This is the office . . .'

'The office . . .'

'For now.'

'You have a public phone in the hallway. Keeping the overheads down. Very good.'

'Don't get angry.'

'I'm not angry. Don't tell me I'm angry.'

'All right. You're not angry.'

I counted the banknotes, folded them, put the wad in my pocket.

He put a cheap mint sweet in his mouth and leant against the table with his arms folded.

'What a stupid place to hide cash. It would take me thirty seconds to find it.'

Alfie pushed the mint into one cheek so he could speak.

'Ah, but that's *you*, Harry. You're going to see me through this safely. I know it.' He was grinning at me again.

He was afraid, but he was grinning. Had he glanced in a mirror he would have jumped. I was getting used to his behaviour. I wasn't jumping.

I turned away to look into the street. Alfie's 'office' was a basement cluttered with boxes of cheap household ornaments, old clothes and broken electrical appliances. There was a mongrel framed in the upper part of the window. It was chewing a plastic bottle. The mongrel was grinning, too.

The grinning dog made me decide that I would get a gun, but I would not tell Alfie I had it. I would make a point of refusing anything he might bring home. You can't be too careful.

He took a bottle of Scotch from the floor of a large wardrobe and poured us both a generous two fingers. This bottle of Scotch had walked out of a bonded warehouse by itself and had knocked on Alfie's door. He felt I should know that. It would give it more of a kick. He liked to be seen to consume perks, to be party to a greater communal enjoyment. A priest in fancy sunglasses comes to mind.

He was working hard to pass off his drinking as such. He must have seen something in my face. He went to the kitchen to fill a milk jug with water, and to get ice from the fridge.

'Sorry, I've no ginger,' he said. He knew I didn't

drink whisky with ginger. He was trying to make out that we were having a sociable drink.

'Water and ice,' I said. 'That will be fine.'

The jug hit the glass hard. The water slopped into it. He squeezed two ice cubes from his fist.

'Look, I meant to say thanks for digging me out of that situation in the pub,' he said.

'Don't embarrass me now.'

'No – straight up.'

'You already thanked me.'

'No, but really, Harry. I appreciate what you're doing for me. Sit down.'

I didn't want to sit down. I leant against the arm of the couch.

'Leaving your old man at short notice, you really . . .'

'Shut up, Alfie.'

'You know the pressure I'm under. Some fucker poisons me and *I* get investigated.' He dropped clumsily into the one easy chair. 'That can't be right.'

'You want an opinion on that?'

He laughed. The laugh went on a little too long.

'Tell me about Holland,' I said.

'Did you notice his eyes – how slowly they move?'

'Slow eyes . . .'

'Don't be fooled. They only appear to be slow. He doesn't need to read what's coming out of your mouth. He has already been there, and you're thinking he's not up to speed. You're thinking he's not paying attention. He has been there and he knows what he needs to know.'

'I'll try to remember.'

'Nothing slow about Sydney.'

'You speak from experience?'

'He likes to sing sentimental songs.'

'Sings for his friends?'

'He rolls up his tie as he sings. Rolls it into a tight little tube under his chin.'

Now what was it that made me think I never wanted to hear this man sing?

'You get invited to his house parties?'

'I've heard him sing hymns after dinner. People hear him sing "All Things Bright and Beautiful" and they think he's soft. Another mistake.'

'I'm sure he hasn't been singing much of late.'

'Oh but he has. The voice is a little softer, the tie rolled tighter. It makes me nervous watching him.'

'He expects a miracle.'

'He wants action.'

'I don't want to add to his burden.'

'You're here, aren't you?'

'He wants us to do something rash.'

There was no response. A darkness crossed Alfie's face.

'Are we going to be rash, Alfie?'

Kidnapping. Threats. Strong-arm stuff. We were more than capable. I didn't need to say it aloud. A plain-clothes policeman looking for trouble – that was the reputation Alfie liked and felt he deserved. It was simple and endlessly renewable. However, his suspension meant reduced accountability and, curiously, reduced accountability rattled him.

He stroked his nose. There was no grin, but he gave the impression that he would have broken into song had he been able to remember the lyrics. A softly sung ballad to show that he was Sydney's champion.

'Let's go through the facts,' he said after a long silence. He looked around for the bottle.

He began by listing some of our employer's clients. By any measure it was an impressive list. Rock stars, television personalities, politicians, cabaret artists, actors, a hugely successful embezzler, small people pushed into the limelight for a roasting. He then told me that this man was the angriest person he had ever met. How, I wondered, had the singing Sydney Holland given vent to his fierce rage?

He gave me an edited factual account of the disappearance and subsequent fruitless search. For some considerable time after he remained absorbed in that which he chose to withhold.

Alfie searched for a video tape, fumbled with it until he got it into the machine on the floor, rummaged on his knees for the remote control.

'Just play it,' I said impatiently. He looked pathetic lurching about on his knees. 'Press the button on the machine.'

'Yes, of course,' he said, and did so immediately. He was embarrassed that it had not occurred to him to do so. He stood up hurriedly. He showed me the recorded television appeal the husband had made, the images that had been analysed by the psychologist.

'What are you looking at me like that for?' He was about to tilt the contents of his glass into his mouth. 'Don't worry about this,' he said, looking into the glass, 'it's under control.'

I nodded and sat down.

'Good,' he said. He struck a pose that suggested he

was determined to remain standing. 'Now – do you want to see that again?'

I shook my head. I had to endure the spectacle of him pouring the contents of his glass back into the bottle.

'When this is over, Harry, I'm taking a holiday. You should come with me. I'm not talking about fishing on a lake. A real holiday. New York. What do you say? There's an aircraft carrier at the end of Forty-Sixth Street. You can hire it for parties.'

'You're talking like a fruit, Alfie, and I'm tired.'

He began to laugh. He laughed so hard he had to sit down. He retrieved his drink from the bottle without realising he was doing it. Then, he told me his wife, Ruth, had thrown him out. He looked up at me with eyes that betrayed a genuine incredulity.

'I'm sorry to hear that, Alfie,' I said. I saw him waver and he became emotional. His eyes smarted and his lip began to tremble. I didn't know how to cope with this. A hand on the shoulder just wasn't enough. Telling him that there was a function in being sad seemed hopelessly glib. I repeated his name. Repeating his name sounded to my ears like a clumsy attempt to wake a man from a stupor.

He quickly regained his composure.

'She threw me out because of the suspension. Because I took a little extra – for us. I squeezed a few sleazy gets.' His eyes were downcast now. He was watching his words fall out of his mouth and make a filthy mess on the floor.

'She didn't know about the extra?'

'Of course she didn't know. What do you take me for?'

'You're a disgraced copper, Alf. I'm getting tired of telling you that.'

'Yes-yes. And you're my pal.'

'I'm here, aren't I? And I am sorry to hear you've split with your wife.'

'Thank you,' he said formally.

'This is a dump,' I said. 'We'll have to get you a better place.'

He was looking at me again. 'I called to the house. She won't open the door. She read me a letter she was going to send to me. She read it to me through the door.'

Ruth was an out-of-work cellist. By any measure, she and Alfie were an unlikely match. There had to have been something special between them. A mysterious, private connection of which I had always been jealous. He painted me a picture of her sitting alone in their house with her cello after reading to him through the hall door.

'Can you imagine how I felt?'

'No.' I couldn't imagine how he felt because I couldn't quite believe his account.

'Damn right you can't. "Dear Alfie" – *through the door.* Does this happen to other people?'

'It sounds normal to me.' That's what I said. It wasn't what I was thinking. I refused to believe their private connection had been entirely broken with Alfie's fall from grace.

'Normal,' he exclaimed.

'First alimony payment I made I posted through the letter-box in twopenny pieces.'

'Oh Jesus.'

'Heard it rolling up the floorboards in the hall.'

'Christ. What sort of a person are you?'

'Appalling, isn't it?'

'Jesus Christ.' There was a short pause. 'You loved her, though?'

'Yes-yes.'

'And you still do?'

I didn't dare answer.

'I was poisoned, too, you know,' I said. 'I first met my wife in a vegetarian restaurant. She thought I was a vegetarian. In fact, I was recovering from a bout of food poisoning . . .'

My voice trailed off. Suddenly, I was very tired.

I leant forwards, balancing a phantom weight on my back – my father's familiar profile. I patted Alfie on the shoulder.

'Jesus Christ,' he said, his spirits lifting, 'the people in my life . . .' He was shocked at me with my bag of small change.

The sound of coins rolling on varnished floorboards filled my head; that, and my own voice, curiously faint, angrily calling my wife's name through the letter-box.

I lay on my back on the lumpy box couch and gazed at the cheap lampshade that hung in the middle of the room. It was suspended several inches too low. I had an impulse to spring to my feet and smash it against the ceiling with a single blow. Instead, I laid perfectly still. I heard the water men dig up the road in another city. I heard a corncrake cry across a distant lake. Nothing was right. There was trouble ahead, but there was still time to walk away cleanly. The hotel job would be enough. Sorry for your trouble, Sydney. To hell with you, Alfie.

I re-ordered my dinner. Had the fish instead of the cutlets. Then, I re-arranged the recent past. I ignored

Alfie on the lake shore, cast my line, caught a fish, cooked it for the old man's supper.

It was cold out on the lake. I got the shivers. I shook so violently I thought I might capsize the boat.

'Wake up, Harry,' Alfie's voice boomed. He must have been using the lampshade as a megaphone. 'It's time to go to work.'

Chapter 6

'Is there any coffee?' I asked.

'Yes. Of course there's coffee.'

I ate an orange over the sink. There was cold coffee in an espresso pot left over from a previous life. It smelt like piss. Alfie heated it on the stove and we drank it. I looked about me. Another room without prospects. No one to lick my face. I slid my hand under my shirt, scratched my stomach. My own cynicism had made me lazy. My laziness had made me predictable. I had to do something about that.

The telephone rang in the hall as we were leaving.

'Don't answer it,' Alfie said.

'I wasn't going to,' I said, a little indignant. 'Why the hell would *I* answer it?'

It was 5.30 a.m. There was a sour smell in the car. I felt entitled to be a little indignant.

'There's something about Mr Holland that bothers me,' I said, before he turned over the engine.

He laughed. 'Just the one thing?'

'He didn't appear to be listening.'

'What are you talking about?'

'He just wanted to say his piece.'

'The man's daughter is missing. This one we're going to watch – his son-in-law – has something to do with it. You think he shouldn't be distracted?'

'What I said is, he wasn't listening.'

'Mr Holland's ears are legendary.'

'He likes gossip?'

'Liking it is neither here nor there.'

'Nothing escapes his legendary ears?'

'He hears all the showbiz gossip and a lot more besides.'

'He wasn't listening.'

'Sydney has a man burn the hairs out of his ears with cotton wool soaked in alcohol. People who know that think he's vain. I know it's because he can hear that little bit better.'

'Is that a fact?'

'This man lights the soaked cotton wool on a stick and paints Holland's ears with it. It's a Turkish thing.'

'I know it's a Turkish thing,' I said stupidly.

Alfie threw his head back and let out a loud guffaw. He put his foot down on the accelerator. I still could not let go –

'You saw the roll of money . . .'

'Will you shut up about Holland.'

'You noticed he didn't look at the bill. He just peeled off some notes.'

'Shut it, Harry.'

'I don't like him, Alfie.'

Alfie put on a woozy tape. The road ahead was clear. He put his foot to the floor.

'I'm just looking out for us,' I said, as I was flung back into the seat. My recollection is that all the traffic lights were green en route to Waterloo Station. In the station I bought the newspapers and a bunch of bananas. Alfie retrieved a package from a locker. The package contained a fancy pair of binoculars with a night-sight facility, and a pair of walkie-talkies. There were other items, which were wrapped. He returned these to the locker. Equipment he had filched, I assumed. A personal store used unofficially when, officially, there could be no legal surveillance. Equipment used to get close, not to collect hard evidence. Holland had made me uneasy but secretly I was glad to be on a job with my crooked friend.

The early morning light pricked my eyes with little injections of goodwill and humanity as we sped along by the river towards Chelsea. A dustbin lorry moving like a tank at full throttle forced Alfie to slow down. The Peace Pagoda in Battersea Park on the far bank leant out over the river to watch us pass. Alfie blasted the windscreen with soapy water jets and switched on the wipers at full tilt to wash away the dust from the bin lorry.

'Maybe she *is* alive,' I mumbled.

'We'll see,' he said, and pulled out dangerously from behind the lorry.

It was strange being back in London. My past did not seem to matter. There had been a clerical error and I had been given the freedom of the city.

Travelling alone in a car I like to talk to dead friends. Travelling with Alfie at the wheel I didn't hear dead friends. They were in another place, filling the kettle, expecting me to visit.

We were a little behind on our schedule. Alfie tore up the wrong side of the road and with great precision pulled back into lane just in time to avoid a pedestrian island. Was he being reckless? I was suffering from an excess of moderate behaviour.

Alfie's new-found confidence, however, was a worry.

There were people making trouble for him and I needed to keep out of the way. Did he understand that? I put the point to him. He told me he had nothing to worry about and I was to keep my mind on the job. He appreciated my concern. Was touched by it.

'They won't fire me,' he said. 'I'm needed. Other people need people like you. It's a fact. Am I right, Harry?'

Suddenly, the world was very crowded.

'I've finished with all of that, Alfie. I told you.'

'Sure you have.'

'No. Really. I've quit.' My voice was dropping progressively. It was getting smaller. Icier.

'If you say so.'

'You're not listening to me . . .'

'I'm deaf and dumb, Harry. I'm a fool for even mentioning it.'

There was a long silence. We were back on schedule. Alfie drove responsibly. Then, he glanced at me with a leading grin.

'I hear you,' he said. 'When you want to make a point you lower your voice. I have a tendency to shout – master of the sudden bark. You haven't noticed?'

'Now when do I get to see you bark?'

There was another silence; this one shorter. He seemed disappointed at my response, but rallied conspicuously. 'I've learnt a lot from you,' he said.

'Have you?' I said in a very small voice.

'I know what you're doing – you look at me and you decide I need a friend who tells me I'm a villain. That way you can show you're a true friend. Have you any idea how much that means to me?'

His grin was so broad now that cat-piss breath was leaking from the corners of his mouth.

I kept my mouth shut.

He swung into a side street.

'Now that you have more time you might get a game at the airport,' he ventured. 'Always a hell of a match. What do you say?'

He took another turn. The car lurched over a set of sleeping policemen. He misjudged the speed for clearance on the first one. I thought the exhaust might be ripped off. Something underneath made contact, but Alfie didn't give a damn. Solly would have been appalled at my choice of friends.

He parked the car some way down the street from the house. When he switched off the engine the tape machine stopped.

'Relax,' he said, identifying the house with a jab of his index finger. 'He won't be out of there for another forty minutes.'

He was telling *me* to relax. That was rich.

'A man of habit,' he announced. 'You keep watch. I need to shut my eyes for a minute. Ever since I banged my head on the pavement I get this humming when I wake up.' He slid down in his seat. 'I can get it to go away if I concentrate.' He kept his eyes shut and continued. 'Did I tell you about the case we had at the station between Christmas and New Year?'

'No.'

'This villain decided he'd practise free-form with a chair. He broke the desk sergeant's jaw. Wally Preston hit him on the head with his stick. When he woke up, our friend claimed he could only see in black and white. Tried to sue, but got nothing.'

'Are you sure we have the right house?'

'Harry, this is interesting. He said it wasn't the black and white you get with Humphrey Bogart. More leaden. "Everything made out of lead" – his words.'

I slid down in the passenger seat, resigned to my abysmal life.

'Eventually, he won't remember the colour red. He'll just know that tomatoes are red.'

'Wally is now an inspector, I take it?'

'Wally Preston is a hero,' said Alfie with a smirk.

There was a brief pause. Alfie performed some kind of a facial exercise. 'When I say I get a humming in my head from bouncing it on the pavement, really it's more of a buzzing.'

'A buzzing?'

'Yes. A buzzing.'

'What – like a bee?'

'Yes. Like a bee.'

'You should have told me about the buzzing when you interrupted my fishing, Alfie. I would never have agreed to this.'

'I'll tell you something really strange – I don't know whether it was the poison or the bang on the head but I've acquired a sixth sense. I can tell if I'm being watched . . .'

'Alfie . . .'

'I'm serious. I can feel their gaze. It makes my flesh tingle. What do you make of that?'

He still had his eyes shut. He was concentrating.

'Maybe if you got Wally to give you a tap on the head you'd have X-ray vision.'

He gave out a coarse laugh. He told me to keep my eyes on the house.

I slid down further in the seat, chose my moment – 'Holland . . .' I said, as though thinking aloud.

'What about him?' Alfie asked impatiently.

'There's something wrong with him.'

'You don't like his manner.'

'No. I don't like his manner.'

'And you think I give a damn.'

'I'm just looking out for the both of us.'

'The doctor has him on Prozac. There – are you happy?'

'An antique opium bottle – that's more his line.'

'If you say so.'

'You've done him a *big* favour in the past?'

Alfie opened his eyes.

'I've told you.'

'You told me you showed him the psychologist's report and that you've known him for a long time.'

'That's enough about Holland.'

I put my hand up in submission. 'Any friend of yours, Alfie . . . Go back to sleep. Get rid of that buzzing.'

Alfie grunted, closed his eyes again and turned over in his seat. I wound down my window. It was still early in the morning but already there was a warm breeze. It entered the car, did a quick tour of the back seat and left by the way it had come. We sat for five minutes in silence. I extended one hand out of the window, stretched my fingers in the breeze that now ran rings around the car.

'Are you with somebody?' he asked.

'No.'

'Are you after one woman in particular? I mean, is there somebody special?'

'No.'

'You don't have to tell me.'

'I've just told you.'

'I'm just curious, that's all.'

'Well. Now you know.'

'You were married once.'

'Yes.' I wasn't prepared to elaborate.

'There's a lot of superstition in a marriage, don't you think?'

'Of course there is,' I replied without due consideration. 'Are you surprised?'

'A lot of superstition involved in making love to a woman,' Alfie continued.

'You think so?' I said casually. This new observation seemed to make his first proposition altogether more credible.

'Don't you?' he asked.

'No,' I replied. 'What are you talking about?' I knew that for some people superstition was a secret comfort. A convenient explanation for things going wrong. Alfie, however, did not fit the profile. Not by any stretch of the imagination.

He scoffed. 'Never mind,' he concluded. He raised his pair of binoculars, which were slightly larger than opera glasses. He studied the upstairs windows of our target house. I knew that he wanted to talk about his wife, but he was holding back.

'Let me shock you,' he said, speaking out of the side of his mouth. 'A young woman marries this old widower for his money and she tells him she is going to fuck him to death. And that's what she does – she fucks him to death.'

'Call the police.'

'I'm serious.'

'You don't think she just marries an old man with a bad heart and he dies because he can't stand the pace?'

'She tells her friends she is going to do it. Then, she *actually* fucks him to death.'

'You're making this up, aren't you?'

'No. It's true. You ask Holland. He knew the man.'

'*Holland* told you this?' It was my turn to scoff. 'Were his eyes twinkling?'

'Holland didn't tell me. He just knew the man. This is out of the mouth of the coroner. The widow has the house. The money. The lot.'

He gave a short cackle. Alfie's emotions were running away with him. His mind was jumping all over the place. I didn't know what to say to him. Eventually I mumbled, 'Well, if it isn't true, it ought to be.'

That seemed to be a satisfactory response.

'Are you and Ruth finished?' I asked bluntly.

'No,' he said, jerking the binoculars away from his eyes. He seemed genuinely alarmed at my question. 'Harry, you're my friend, so I can talk to you . . .'

I nodded with what I thought might be a wise frown. In any case, it was an expression that suggested he could set aside the superstition crap.

'The money I make,' he said. 'It's for her.'

He was, of course, referring to the extra cash. The backhanders. That was understood.

'I know,' I said, extending my nod.

I was sure that Alfie's extortion activities were more

extensive than he had led me to believe. We both would have been embarrassed were it otherwise.

He would do anything to keep her, he told me. The conviction in his voice told me this was a recent discovery.

'I know you would, Alfie.' What else could I say?

'I come home late on a Saturday afternoon – "I have a bottle of milk and two tomatoes," I tell her. "Where have I been?"

'"You've been to your mother's," she says.

'"I've been at my mother's," I say. But now she's nodding to the living room. There's two of them in there from Internal Affairs. I've just survived being poisoned and my head is singing from concussion and it takes *two* monkeys to tell me I'm suspended pending an investigation. It couldn't wait until Monday, they told me. I caught them looking over the contents of the room.'

'Cut-backs, Alfie. Monkey training isn't what it should be. You know that.'

'No. They wanted me to catch them snooping. What really sickens me is that they made sure Ruth was there for their little speech.' Alfie's eyes were wide open now. Wider than I had ever seen them. He was staring straight ahead. That suited me. I didn't want him staring at me with those projector eyes. He was burning with indignation and with fear.

The indignation I could understand. I was embarrassed for him having been caught red-handed. The fear extended beyond his fate at the hands of any investigative body; beyond the threats from his clumsy enemies. When his fierce stare was directed at the rear-view mirror I opened my door.

80

'The black Citroën, yes?' I blurted out.

'The black Citroën,' he confirmed.

'I'm going to take a look.'

He didn't answer. I got out of the car. Shut the door gently. Took a deep breath and began walking towards the house. The word 'relax' slithered out from a tight little crack located somewhere below my forehead. 'Name me five species of fish you might catch in a lake. Name me three. There – you see. Relax. You're in London helping a pal.'

Toby Harquin, Holland's son-in-law, had found a parking space across the street from his house. The Citroën squatted on the road. A quick inspection of the interior revealed nothing special. A crook lock for the steering wheel under the driver's seat. An ice scraper for the windscreen in the cubby-hole by the steering column. Between the front seats a bar of chocolate with two squares missing. A petrol voucher. A sun-bleached parking ticket. There were a few stones under the foot pedals.

I took my time looking over the house. Toby had the front bedroom windows open and the curtains drawn. Expensive curtains; too heavy to billow in the breeze. There was a marmalade cat on the first-floor wrought-iron balcony. It appeared to be on home territory. I don't like cats. They remind me of Alfie's coffee.

Framed in the sitting-room window was a small marble bust on a plinth. The bust was of an aesthetic, scholarly young man. He was looking out at the street. I didn't like him either. His head was too small. I loosened my walk. I crossed the street so that I could get a look at the basement. The basement window was protected with one of those expanding lift-shaft grills. There was one red boxing glove wedged between it and the window pane. It looked as though it had been there a long time.

I walked around the block. There was no access at the rear of the terrace. I was thinking about the man in Alfie's story as I went on my way. That got me thinking about my father's solitary existence. I thought about him eating his minced meat and carrots. I imagined him staring at sticks of yellowing celery in the pint glass on the table in front of him. I was thinking I should call him to assuage my conscience by arranging another trip of some kind, when I turned back into the street to find that Alfie's car was unoccupied. He had left it unlocked. He had scribbled a note –

On foot – radio

I rummaged for the walkie-talkies. He had taken one. The other he had pushed under the front passenger seat. At first I couldn't get the damn thing to work. I couldn't make the call-out signal. Then, it bleated and Alfie spoke.

'He's just turned on to the King's Road. Walking quickly towards Sloane Square. Probably on his way to the tube station.'

'I'm with you.' I was already running.

A short time later, another bleat.

'Moving faster. He hasn't spotted me. He must be late.'

'Can't see you.'

Alfie kept the channel open. There was a jumble of street sounds and static. These were old models.

'Yes. The station.'

'I'm at the Square,' I panted.

Another short break, then –

'Eastbound platform.'

'With you.'

When I got down on to the eastbound platform, I saw Alfie across the tracks, in a train going west. Toby was in the same carriage. Alfie saw me through the window. I thought he might ignore me, but, instead, he gave me a hearty wave. He was happy to see his old friend Harry. I felt a right idiot waving back.

The train pulled out of the station.

CHAPTER 7

After four days of surveillance we had learnt nothing new. Alfie's couch had turned into a dried-out reptile that got in the way of a good night's sleep. The statue belonging to Toby continued to stare out of his living-room window. I got sick looking at it talk out of the side of its mouth, reporting on what it saw in the street. I was watching Toby give it a haircut when Alfie woke me with a sharp rap on the car window. He was standing on the pavement holding two coffees in polystyrene cups without lids. Had he provided a decent bed and coffee that wasn't piss I would not have fallen asleep on the job.

When he got back into the car I could smell whisky and garlic on his breath.

Three doors up from Toby's house there was a shallow bay window through which a partition was visible. The partition had floral wallpaper and stopped short of the ceiling. It made the room look like a theatre set. I'd seen rooms like this in provincial cities: large terrace mansions reduced to student accommodation; rooms that could not be filled regardless of the amount of cheap boxy furniture thrown into them.

In this neighbourhood a partitioned room seemed out of place; the space compressed to three-quarter scale. What bit of life curled up there each night, I wondered.

Alfie would have told you it was somebody like me.

I could sense him following my eye line as I fixed on another upstairs window further up the street. It had a phosphorous glow.

'There's always one bastard who has a weird light in his room,' he announced. 'He's up there now in his Y-fronts and sunglasses. Perhaps he's got something tied to a chair.'

'You think so?'

'Cuts right across all class, cultural and ethnic groups. Your weird-light man recognises no bounds.'

I tried to stifle a yawn, but it turned into something of a circus act. Alfie had slid down in his seat and would have yawned, but gave the impression he couldn't get his mouth open.

'A couple of weeks ago . . .' he continued, '. . . before all of this . . . I got a call to a house. Somebody I know . . .'

'Oh yeah?'

'Rich bastard. He'd forgotten to switch on his house alarm. When he came home he found a burglar sitting in his favourite chair in the living room . . .'

'And he called *you*?'

'Like I say – he knows me. And he knew this bloke sitting in his chair. And he wants me to come and sort it. This heap of shit in the chair is dead drunk and he starts weeping and wailing. He's a heavy bloke and my friend can't get him out of the house.'

'Alfie, you're lying to me.'

'On this bloke's lap is a lock of Beethoven's hair in a small circular frame with bulbous glass. He's taken it off the wall . . .'

'Beethoven's hair . . .'

'It was all cut off on his deathbed to be kept as souvenirs. How much do you suppose a thing like that is worth?'

'Your friend – he knew this drunk so he called you?'

'Told me it was his cousin. That's why he called me and not the local shop. This heap of shit was sitting there bawling his eyes out, waving at the alarm sensor up in the corner, making the little red light go on and off.'

'You got him out of the chair?'

'I gave him a kicking in the chair, then I nicked him.'

'That wasn't the plan.'

'I fucking hate to see a man in a state like that.'

'Alfie, I'm sitting here patiently. That doesn't mean I'm waiting to hear another of your copper's stories. I'm not interested in your copper's stories. They're all about sad bastards, and that's an imposition.'

He was content with this rebuke. I knew there would be more such stories.

The target – you get to like them or you get to hate them. I knew that much from previous surveillance work. I hadn't yet made up my mind about Toby, and Alfie wasn't interested either way. He was in another place and I wished him well.

Another clammy day. I drank my coffee in three gulps. It began to rain heavily. The rain temporarily enriched the street's jaded colours and darkened the mortar between the bricks. I rolled down the window a little, rested my head against the glass, listened to the splatter and gurgle in the gutters and drainpipes. It had a calming effect, but now I needed a piss.

While I was listening to the drainpipes Alfie put a grubby peppermint in his mouth and followed it with a mouthful of coffee. The fumes from his cocktail of garlic, peppermint and alcohol came out of his nostrils and mingled with the steam from his polystyrene cup. The rain hadn't brought the colour back to Alfie's cheeks. The skin around his eyes was puffy, but his eyes flashed with a fierce intensity. He seized on any distraction. A woman emerged from the house with the theatre set. Alfie locked on to her. He seemed to stop breathing lest it distort his vision. He studied her over the rim of his cup. He remarked on her brassy appearance, her 'cocker spaniel coat'.

The woman hoisted a small, cheap umbrella, stepped into the street and began making her way in our direction. She was wearing teenager's costume jewellery, Alfie noted. 'She has five children and plays the accordion in the kitchen,' he told me.

She was soon followed by a middle-aged man in an expensive coat. The rain splattered on the bald dome of his head – I was sure I could hear the droplets drumming on his skull. He had a little nest of grey curls at the back of his neck that appeared to have been created by the wind eddies in his wake. He had a brisk, civil servant's walk.

'They've had sex,' Alfie declared, still not having drawn breath. 'I can tell. I'm never wrong about that.'

'She's his wife,' I said without conviction.

'No she's not.'

'She's the cleaner, then.' As I've said, I was bored.

'Most people shouldn't be allowed to lay a finger on another person.'

'Why is that?'

'Imagine that pair coupling,' he gasped. 'Imagine the result. People like that should have to sit an exam before shaking hands with each other.'

Alfie was doing a bad job concealing his despair but he was breathing again, and soon he had returned to the subject of his wife.

Toby was a businessman. He had two shady investment companies with registered offices in Soho and Primrose Hill. Both companies invested in entertainment. That covered just about everything from pornography to commemorative mugs. His father-in-law had described him as a wife-beater, a ruthless gangster and a degenerate. Toby did a lot of work from home. He was a very busy man who was not socialising.

The publicist's description notwithstanding, he presented the profile of a man unable to change his life; a man caught in the day his wife disappeared; a man denying himself pleasure because he could not share it with his missing loved one. There was nothing surprising in this. Most people with a missing loved one would recognise such behaviour. But Toby was also a man who knew he was being watched.

He contacted the police every day for an update on the investigation. He maintained daily contact with his father-in-law. The possibility that his wife had climbed out from under his regime and had simply run off seemed more credible with each passing day. However, I was the only one who thought so.

Alfie had already dismissed this out of hand.

'Run off with somebody else,' I suggested. 'You can see he's like you, Alf. You can see he's a control nut.'

That was the wrong thing to say. Alfie didn't see the irony. He didn't see I was pointing the finger at both of us. Our respective plans for personal salvation amounted to sitting on our hands.

He just got irritated. The wicked joy was absent in his eyes. It was almost as though he was sorry for his badness and under the circumstances that was not healthy.

Late on the following night Toby got into a car with two well-dressed thugs and they went collecting. At first we weren't sure what they were at, but we got close enough to observe one visit. Toby sat down with the management of a Brixton club over a bottle of cheap wine. He had shares in the club, or he was running a protection racket, or he was laundering money. My judgement of it was that he was laundering. In any case, it gave me the opportunity to further reprimand my copper friend for being a crook.

'There now, Alf, that's how the big boys do it. You were only in the ha'penny place.'

'Shut your mouth. You don't know what's going on. It's not house money. I know the management. I know the owners. He's banking.'

'You sure?'

'Laundering drug money.'

'You sure? You could check with the vice squad.'

'Get off my case, Harry.'

'Notice he hasn't touched his glass of wine. I bet he has one of the monkeys take a sip of every drink before he touches it. I bet even Toby there has heard about your glass of good cheer.'

'I want a look inside the house,' I told Alfie.

'Breaking and entering.'

'I've had a look at the locks. I can open the door.'

'Well then . . .'

'I'll need a set of picks.'

'In the boot. There's a repair kit. In the bag with the jump-leads.'

It was Friday. Toby left the house early that evening. He was dressed up and we had no idea where he was going or how long he would be away. He might have been going to the Arts Club for dinner. He might have been going to feed Vanessa a crust through a hole in a metal door.

In any case, Alfie shifted into the front passenger seat so that he had a clear view to one end of the street. He then adjusted the rear-view mirror so that he could see both corners at the other end. He then tested the walkie-talkies.

'The alarm – if he's switched it on –'

'Yes, I know,' I said cutting in.

'And for God's sake, put it back together properly before you leave.'

'Please . . .'

'Off you go, then . . .'

The set of picks had me worried. He must have got them in a Christmas cracker at the policemen's ball. Fortunately, Toby had nothing too sophisticated barring my way, though the door was heavy and had hinge bolts, and the frame was reinforced with a London bar.

As an understrapper I had broken down my life into compartments so that I could behave differently in each. That was the theory, and the theory gave an edge to the sense of importance needed to carry out the routine and the trivial. When housebreaking, I was a housebreaker whose focus was absolute. All points met on the target. There was no possibility of straying. There was no sweating or shivering. No sense of having been abandoned by my masters and no fear of being trapped. On entering the premises I would stand for a moment to listen and to adjust to the dimensions, then I would be on my way, moving through the narrowest of ethereal corridors knowing that soon I would cease to be a housebreaker.

This, however, was different. There was no specific target. This was a snoop mission. The focus would be no less intense, but it would be constantly shifting. Bringing the walkie-talkie into Toby Harquin's house was at Alfie's insistence. He had rigged each with an earpiece and clip microphone. I wasn't comfortable with it but the alternative was to have him meddling while I disabled the alarm, and then lurking at the window; or, worse still, have him lumbering around in my wake.

The house was warm. It was also partially lit. Toby was in the habit of leaving on some lights when he went out and when he went to bed. In the hall I was immediately struck by the lack of air circulation.

Evidently, Toby didn't know windows could open or, if he did, he was afraid that once opened they could not be shut again.

Perhaps he just wanted to keep what was left of his wife's presence trapped in the house. Heartbroken relatives and domestic killers alike sometimes do such a thing.

I listened. I could hear the low hum of the fridge in the basement kitchen. It was a house with most of its interior doors left ajar. I took two small wedges from my pocket, the only relics from my previous existence. I had carried these in my pocket out on the lake. I had idly slid one over the other in my pocket to comfort me while I sprawled on Alfie's couch. Now, I jammed them between the door and the frame.

There were expensive Persian rugs placed one next to another throughout the ground floor. Rich reds, blues and greens. A tight-weave carpet on the staircase with thick underfelt. The walls in the hall and the stairwell were painted the cream I associated with new council houses in the 1960s. There was a clutter of oil paintings and etchings. The impression was that they were there in temporary storage.

There were three chandeliers on the ground floor, all too big for the interiors they lit. One hung in the hall. One in the small living room which opened on to the small dining room, where the third hung over a circular mahogany table that was slightly askew. Beyond the table the branches of a juniper bush rubbed against the glass of the sash window which overlooked the cramped back yard.

The hall light was on but the living room and the

dining room were illuminated only by the spill from the hall. Standing between the living room and the dining room, I filled my lungs with the lifeless air. Under the smell of wealthy gangster I caught what I thought must be a trace of Vanessa. Such was the stagnation I sensed that the trace would grow perceptively the closer my nose was to the floor.

'Well?'

'I'm in, aren't I?'

'Did you wipe your feet?'

'Yes, Ma.'

'Harry, I'm so glad you're helping me out . . .'

'Will you shut up about that. It's an embarrassment.'

'You've nothing to worry about in there. I'm looking out for you.'

'Yes. Well just do that. I'm not lonely. You don't have to keep me company.'

'You know what? I feel a lot better now. I feel I've got that stuff out of my system. I've sweated it out and it's not going to give me cancer.'

'Really . . .' I found myself squatting and drawing another slow, deep breath.

'Yes. And maybe I'm the stronger for it.'

'You think they knew what they were doing with the dose they gave you?'

'No. They wanted me dead. You look at these people and you see the hate, but still – something like this comes as a shock . . . Now I tell everybody I'm lucky.'

'I never like *lucky*.'

'You plan . . . you make provision . . . but – have you any idea how much I've paid into my pension fund?'

'No. I haven't.'

'A lot.'

'Really?' I rose from my crouch.

'Are you on a pension plan?'

'No.'

'A man in your line of work needs a good pension plan, Harry. You'll make a sad old man. You'll need cash.'

I was looking at the bust now. Looking at the back of its head. It was staring at the heavy curtains that were drawn two feet in front of it. I thought it might turn slowly on its plinth to look at me.

'Pension funds. Now there's a missed opportunity for a man with your scruples,' I said.

'Don't I know it. Does that stop me from contributing? No. It does not. I know what's good for me. I'm not going to be a sad old fucker. Ruth and me – we'll have more than enough.'

'Be quiet for a minute, will you?'

I turned slowly myself, three hundred and sixty degrees. Had the two clairvoyants moved through the house as I was now doing? Had Toby let them in? If he had let them in, had it been together or separately? Had they conjured visions that were contradictory? In my experience malevolent and cunning people were often superstitious and always believed in extraordinary manipulative powers, whatever their source.

Perhaps I had been misled. Perhaps Toby had been misrepresented to me. He might be a warm, sensitive human being whose wife had been abducted.

'Well?'

'Well what?'

'Anything?'

'If I need a copper – I'll call you.'

I began to pick through papers that were stored in an ornamental box under a sideboard.

'All quiet out here,' he said, while he thought about what next to bring up.

For all his experience, I think he was nervous. Afraid that I might be as clumsy as he would be.

'I asked Sydney about the first time he saw his son-in-law behaving badly. He told me it was at the child's fifth birthday party . . .'

'I'm busy.'

'No – this will interest you . . . For his child's fifth birthday party Toby hired a clown. The house was full of kids and their parents, and after Vanessa dished out the birthday cake the clown did his stuff. Meanwhile, Toby slipped out to run a business errand. When he came back he swung his daughter around and around, then he took the clown aside and said, "A little voice tells me you weren't funny."

'"How do you mean?" says the clown.

'"When I was a kid," Toby says, "every clown was funny. I've always liked the circus. Full of people good at doing the one thing. Now, you've disappointed me. Now, I can't rely on the circus to entertain me and my family."'

'Alfie – really . . . these stories . . .'

'Sydney told me he thought it was a joke until Toby refused to pay the clown, and when Sydney stepped in to pay, Toby flew into a rage. He stuffed money into the clown's mouth then slapped him out of the house.'

'Did all the kids laugh?' I asked wearily.

'Harry, don't mock.'

'I blame the little girl.'

'The man's unstable. They're all like that, these fuckers, and we have a wife-killer here. So get on with what you're at.'

I descended into the basement. The hum of the fridge seemed unnecessarily loud. I thought it might be empty and that would account for the loudness. I opened it. It was filled with prepared meals in Waitrose carrier bags. Cartons of skimmed milk, low-fat yoghurt and bags of cold meat. On the floor behind me was a large tin of the best olive oil, in a Harrods Food Hall bag. There was a full wine rack on one wall. A stack of bills held in a bulldog clip. I found a notebook with handwritten recipes. Alfie had shown me several letters Vanessa had sent to her father hinting at her unhappiness. The recipes were in her hand. They all followed the one format. Ingredients listed first, with quantities. Underneath, clear instructions. Each instruction to a separate line. Each leading word begun with a capitalised letter. It suggested a patient and meticulous person.

There was a lot of stale bread. All the cereal boxes and biscuit packets were opened. There was a pile of unwashed dishes in the sink.

I went upstairs. On the first floor was a second sitting room, which doubled as a home office. There was a roll-top desk in one corner. It was cluttered with business correspondence and statements from an impressive array of commercial and merchant banks. Near one of the two windows overlooking the street was a computer which was set up on a lacquered oriental table. Access to computer files required a password, so I didn't waste my time with it. I examined this room; the daughter's bedroom; and two others.

'Your friend Sydney . . .' I said, as I looked under one of the spare beds.

I could hear Alfie swallow. What had he got down there? Hip flask? Where did he keep that?

'. . . Does he talk to his son-in-law – keep his enemy close, sort of thing?'

'They talk. Of course they talk.'

'Talking with Toby – that's what has him convinced he's harmed her?'

'Yes. And we're making doubly sure.'

'Yes. You've told me.'

'Sydney likes you.'

'No, he doesn't.'

'You're one of the gifted.'

'He's a PR man.'

'I talked to him, you see. Told him you were the best. We were invited to dinner so that he could be doubly sure.'

I heard him take another swig. I concluded that he wasn't trying to hide his drinking. He needed the full charge a hip flask offered.

'Don't drink on the job, Alf.'

'I'm not drinking,' he said cheerily, 'I'm talking to you. But we can go for a drink later, if you need one.'

'No thanks.'

'We'll visit one of my green rooms.'

'I wouldn't like that.'

Another little swig.

'Where are you?'

'Top landing.'

I entered the master bedroom. The curtains had not been drawn. There were no lights switched on but there was sufficient illumination from the street lamps below for me to see my way. The adjacent bedroom had been converted to a bathroom, and a door knocked through.

'There's a *dizygotheca* in the window of that front bedroom . . .'

'Oh yes?'

'The leaves are turning brown. Shouldn't be in that room. The air is too dry.'

He was using his fancy binoculars.

'Legendary copper, fishing expert and now, plant doctor?'

'Green fingers, Harry. Is it on a tray of pebbles?'

'Yes.'

'Are they dry?'

'Yes.'

'Ah – you see – *she* knew a *dizygotheca* needs to be on a tray of wet pebbles. He doesn't.'

'I'll leave a note.'

'I'll take you to my allotment.'

'Your what?'

'I have an allotment. I keep it a secret. I go there sometimes.'

I was looking at Vanessa's things. Her clothes in the wardrobe. Her cosmetics. I filled my lungs. I didn't need to crouch to catch her smell. It was strong. Seemingly, Toby had left everything belonging to his wife untouched.

'Can't see you with an allotment.'

'Ah well – that's where you're wrong . . .'

'What do you have in the ground? Buried treasure?'

'Vegetables, you bastard.'

'Alfie, you're an empire builder, and that's a fact.'

'Christ. He's back.'

I glanced down into the street. I saw the black Citroën pulling into the kerb twenty yards up from where Alfie was parked.

'Is there another way out, Harry?'

'Basement door at the front.'

'No time. The roof?'

'No access.'

I was already moving speedily down the stairs.

'His daughter is with him.'

Clearly, he had travelled no further than Victoria Station.

'Three doors away. Christ, Harry . . .'

'Do nothing. Sit tight.' I switched off the walkie-talkie.

I had a choice. I could remove the wedges and hide; let them come in and, when they had settled in the living room or the kitchen, take my chances walking down the hall. Or, I could let him turn the keys in the door and trust that the wedges would hold. Presumably, he would go down to the basement and enter that way. I would have time to leave. I chose the latter option.

I got to the door just as he inserted the mortise key. I positioned myself in the corner and, with my foot, held in place the wedge that was jammed between the door and the threshold. There was a gilded cage for catching the letters, not a solid box. An open letter-box flap would give a view of much of the hall. I creased at the spine and pushed myself as far into the corner as I could get.

The mortise lock was opened. The Yale lock was released. The door would not give. Their voices were clear, even through the heavy door. I made my breathing shallow. My eyes fixed on the second wedge, the one I was unable to reach. Toby worked the locks again to ensure that their mechanisms moved freely. He quickly lost his temper and attempted to force the door. Then, when that failed, the letter-box opened. The flap had a strong spring. It yielded with an unnerving scale of tuneless notes. Toby's eyes were inches from my extended leg.

I stared down at the foot that was holding one wedge in place. It was beginning to look like the leg and the foot belonged to somebody else. Then, I had an alarming thought; I turned my head slowly to look up the hall – was I reflected in any surface visible from the letter-box?

The front wall of my stomach rubbed against the back when I saw the hideous little yegg that was me reflected in a china vase. There was nothing I could do but remain absolutely still.

If he saw me he covered well. He got furious. The letter-box flap snapped shut. He repeated his opening of the locks and pushed ever more violently. His daughter whined at his incompetence. The wedge I had inserted in a higher, upright position slipped out of place. The other held. With the help of the foot on the end of the leg and the violent pushing from outside, only now had it fully bit into its task.

Finally, he went to the basement door. I could hear him curse as he searched for the key to unlock the padlock on the railing gate. I removed the secured wedge, picked up the other and let myself out as Toby and his daughter came up the basement stairs to the hall.

I had not reset the alarm. There hadn't been time. This didn't worry me unduly. A man with Toby's temperament was liable to thump himself on the side of the head just as a reminder that next time he should switch it on before leaving the house. And if he was sure he had switched it on — what conclusion could he draw? He could conclude that there had been an intruder. A snoop.

We could live with that.

By the time Toby swung his hall door on its hinges and had stepped out on to his doorstep, I was some considerable distance along the pavement on the opposite side of the street, moving away from Alfie in the car.

CHAPTER 8

Toby spent all of Saturday with his daughter. He went shopping with her on the King's Road. He bought her clothes. He took her to lunch at The Man in the Moon. He let her drink from his glass of lager. She behaved moodily, but was at ease with him. She wasn't bothered by his hand on her shoulder, and on two occasions he managed to make her laugh.

That night we left Toby at his home computer. His portfolio of investments more than eclipsed his two registered companies. There had to be a lot of homework in that. Alfie and I went on a binge. I saw it coming. I thought it best to let Alfie blow.

By 9.00 p.m. we had had plenty. He took me to the pub where they had poisoned him.

'This is where they did it,' he said to me, as he barged open the door. He pushed on through the crowd. He towed me by the sleeve as though I were a recalcitrant child. I saw his presence register on the faces of the bar staff and several of the regular patrons.

'This is a mistake, Alfie,' I muttered.

'Don't they know it, Harry.'

He pushed ever deeper into the crowd. Everyone, it seemed, was party to a primitive tribal conspiracy. There were the select few whose task was to exhibit their barefaced hatred. They swam effortlessly back and forth through the rest, their eyes fixed on us. Evidently, nobody was sorry for what had happened to poor Alfie. They were just a little surprised to see him on his feet. That kind of surprise is always muted and usually manifests itself in sneers designed to point up the temporary nature of the subject's good fortune.

The truth was that Alfie cut a pathetic figure. Had the management not been so busy serving customers they would have had the staff queue to spit in his face. Christ, I thought as my eyes bounced from one monkey to another, this is my reward. The fucker wants a repeat performance. He wants me to save him again.

What a fool I was to fret. Alfie was in control this time. Alfie was in charge. He was watching out for both of us.

When we reached the bar he ordered two drinks. They didn't serve us, of course. The manager attended in person – a walrus man. You can never tell with his sort. They can back down when you least expect it, or they can set about making a clumsy job of cutting your throat. This one leant over the counter, sniffed Alfie, curled his lip.

'I'm thirsty, Joe,' Alfie said, staring him down. 'We're both thirsty. You can see us right, can't you, Joey-boy?'

That was when the sneering turned to sniggering. Alfie quietly put a Centennial .38 Special on the counter. That tightened a few arseholes. The sniggering stopped. Patrons in the immediate vicinity fell silent and shrank enough to provide landing space for a cluster of guardian angels.

Alfie glowered at each man and woman in turn.

'Police,' he growled. He included me in his declaration with a jerk of his thumb.

The silence spread back through the crowd, becoming progressively more polite until it reached those who could not see what was happening; until there was the perception that somebody was about to make a speech. I looked at the hammerless revolver on the counter – certainly not police issue – and I thought, all right, Alfie must have heard me call him stupid and liked it. He wants me to save him again. He's been spoiling for a bit of theatre and I haven't noticed. He puts his hand on the gun and I put my hand on his hand and that's an end to it.

'You see,' he said to me in a low, even voice, 'I've learnt my lesson. I didn't bark.'

He made a show of pulling a flat bottle of Scotch from an inside pocket.

'Two glasses, please, Joey.'

Neither the gun nor the bottle got us the two glasses. With an unsteady hand Alfie reached over the counter and took two straws from a dispenser. I could have had the revolver off the counter and in my pocket in an instant, but I let it sit. I turned my back on the bar, rested my elbows on the counter, glowered at each patron in our immediate company. It was madness, but the wicked joy had returned to Alfie's eyes.

He said he was going to ask some questions. There would be no answers, of course, just as there had been no drinks served and no glasses provided. But that wasn't the point. As I have indicated, my damaged friend Alfie and I were on a binge.

Three nights later Alfie was lying in hospital. He had been pushing himself too hard and now he was lying in a six-bed ward with a purple face, recovering from a heart attack. The purple face was a good deal more than a measure of his embarrassment. As for the drying-out process, it seemed to require that he held his breath.

'Did you see that, Harry?' he repeated in a gasp. 'The ambulance crew were wearing body armour.'

'We were in the wrong neighbourhood,' I told him. We had gone to another of the dumps Alfie frequented and we were getting ready to leave. He had suggested we finish with brandies in the green room of a West End theatre, one of his favourite after-hours haunts. It happened suddenly, or so it seemed to me. He clutched the bar, struck the counter with his forehead, then collapsed into my arms.

'That can't be right,' he said to me, lying in his hospital bed. He made a frail circular motion with one hand in front of his chest.

'You just keep your mouth shut and do as you're told.' I was more shocked at his heart attack than he. 'Nice spot you have here,' I said. 'You can see out the window and you can see the television set. You want me to contact your colleagues on the force? I'm sure they could organise a bunch of flowers in a vase. Maybe they'll feel sorry for you. Drop the investigation.' I was shocked and I was angry. How dare he have a heart attack.

A bright voice came from behind me – 'He slept well last night.'

I turned to find a jolly, Reverend type in pyjamas the colour of Alfie's face.

'Very good,' I muttered.

'We're well looked after in here, aren't we?'

Alfie grunted.

'He's on the mend,' the neighbour continued. 'I've asked.' He was giving exaggerated nods of encouragement, trying in vain to make direct contact with Alfie. If he stopped nodding was he going to wiggle his ears?

I nodded back, returned his happy grin, and turned again to Alfie.

'It's like being in a bad radio play,' he declared, in what I can only describe as a harsh stage whisper.

'How do you explain this mess you've got us into?' I asked stupidly.

'I don't feel qualified to give an answer,' he replied. He was grinning at me, but he was holding his breath. Getting more purple in the face.

'I'm out of here tomorrow,' he said. 'First thing.'

'Don't be ridiculous.'

He beckoned me closer, pointed to the jolly, Reverend type. 'See him. He's a pervert.'

'Is he?'

'He is.'

'What about it?'

'You know me, Harry. I don't mind perverts. It's *confident* perverts I can't stand.'

He was serious. It was the terrible earnestness of a man drying out.

'You're going nowhere until you're right.'

'You have the car outside?'

'You want me to get a stretcher and a team of monkeys?'

'I can walk. We have a job, remember?'

'Will you listen to yourself.'

'I've got responsibilities.'

'I'll take care of everything.'

He scoffed at this.

'What – you haven't collected this week?' I said. 'Where are your real partners, Alfie? Looking after your interests, no doubt. Have you talked to them recently? I'm sure they're putting something aside for you.'

He fixed me with a hard stare. In a way, this was reassuring. 'I'm talking about Holland's daughter.'

'I'll take care of that.'

'Yes? And who's on the job while you're in here?'

'I said I'll take care of it.'

A weary glottal rattle came from the far corner of the ward.

'Oh dear,' rejoined the neighbour uneasily. 'Do you think he wants a drink?'

'You don't seem to appreciate the seriousness of the situation,' Alfie said, leaning towards me.

His words. Not mine.

'Do you want a drink?' the neighbour called out.

'Did I let them take you into hospital with a gun in your pocket?' I asked softly. 'Did I?'

'How the fuck do I know?' Alfie replied in a low, devious voice. 'I was having a heart attack.'

'You need to get some perspective on this. Do you have a Centennial .38 in your locker there?'

Another scoff. 'No. I don't.'

'No. You don't. You take too much for granted.'

'I'm a policeman. Get me a drink.'

'I said I'd take care of Holland and the Toby-fella. Somebody else can take care of you.'

'I want a drink,' he said through his teeth.

I looked at Alfie's neighbour to see if his ears were

wiggling. I was sure he was about to offer Alfie something from a tall plastic bottle, but had the good sense to look away.

Alfie insisted that he would call Holland to give his regular report. Under no circumstances was I to assume that responsibility. I imagined that brief telephone call. There would be no mention of his heart attack. On a job such as ours the client did not want to hear of your troubles.

'I'm alive, aren't I?' he said emphatically. There could be no arguing with that. Anything short of being dead counted as mild. You could get used to a purple face crying out for a drink. Besides, he was an ugly bastard, anyway.

I was to stay clear of Holland altogether.

'Don't complicate things,' he told me. 'Just keep track of Toby.'

'I said I'm on the case.'

'Keep away from Holland.'

'I heard you.'

I asked him if he wanted me to contact his wife.

'No.'

'You don't want her in here . . . ?'

'I'm out of here just as soon as you get me my medicine.'

He didn't want her to see him in this state. I understood.

'I can get her to give you a call. She'll want to know.' For some reason, I couldn't let it pass.

'If she calls the flat,' he said, 'you tell her I'm out putting things right.'

'You gave her the number – she's called you?'

There was a sad little silence.

'No.'

'Well then. You won't have to worry.'

'No . . .'

'Where are you going?' he asked, when I stood up and turned awkwardly.

'To work.'

He gave me a searching look with his sulphurous, hard-boiled eyes. I gave him a glass of water and stepped out into a corridor full of tall nurses. I turned to give what was a self-conscious salute. The small pieces of him that were masquerading as the whole and incorruptible Alfred joined together momentarily as he gave a jerk of his chin to indicate that I should not delay.

'Goodbye, now,' his neighbour volunteered. There was more nodding.

I had already talked to the duty nurse and then to a senior consultant. Alfie's condition was stable, they had said. I told the consultant about the poisoning. Perhaps the poisoning had damaged Alfie's heart, had set something bad in motion. The consultant gave me a steely, expectant look, as though I might continue by describing how I had measured and administered the dose. Evidently, policemen poisoned with pesticide were not his field of expertise and that was something he should endeavour to conceal.

In any case, he refused to be drawn on whether or not the poisoning might have contributed to the heart attack. There was no history of heart disease in the family, he told me. And where had he got this information? From Alfie, of course. I could hear Alfie's carefully pitched voice of protest – I haven't properly begun to abuse my body and my brain, and you tell me I have a problem.

People wore out. Alfie didn't grasp that fact. Were it not for a programme of sedation he would have been out of the bed five minutes after I had left. He would have been looking for a ten-foot nurse to help him down to the registrar's office where he could sign himself out.

That was what I wanted to believe.

As I descended in the hospital lift I heard a rat singing an unfamiliar libretto in the bottom of the lift shaft. I had sobered up too quickly and now I was paying the price. Otherwise, I would have recognised the piece.

I stepped out into a warm summer evening. The smell of cooked food and exhaust fumes filled my nostrils. I took my fists out of my pockets, flexed my fingers, opened my lungs and inhaled deeply.

I went to a public telephone and rang Solly's number. There would be a delay in returning the car that was sitting at the airport. He wasn't available. I left a brief message with his wife.

I had good reason to stay away from Alfie's wife, but I went to see her. Alfie was sick and she should know, with or without his approval. The attention of an estranged wife seemed to me at the time preferable to that of a sometime protector and drinking partner.

To one side of the hall door there was a circular window with a large china swan framed in it. Alfie had a soft spot for that kind of crap. He had bought it and had set it in the round window. That way he knew he had a home. It was sailing right to left and wore something like a bandit's eyemask. It had its small yellow eyes fixed on me when I knocked on the door.

I knew I would be let in. I did not, however, anticipate the effect it would have on me. I had been too busy thinking about the little kick I was sure she would get. To my shame I did not immediately declare the purpose of my unannounced visit. As I closed the door behind me I saw the zero that was her mouth slacken, and I kissed her. She could not have grasped that she made me live again with the warmth of the breath from her nostrils and the persistence of her tongue.

Her hands were frigid, but only because I had her rocking on her heels. Her hands were frigid, but hers was a firm, velvet embrace.

I wanted to keep her rocking on her heels. We had had a brief assignation: a one-night stand behind Alfie's back. We had both regretted the betrayal and had put it safely behind us. Is that what I thought?

'Harry,' she said, 'what are you doing?'

I could not begin to understand the question, but it was enough to work the leverage in my arms. I held her away from me.

'Ruth, look at you,' I said, and bit my lower lip. I could not yet let go of her completely. To have told her that I was pleased to see her at this point would have been risible. Besides, in the first instance of her setting eyes on me she had glanced over my shoulder to see if Alfie was with me.

Now we pretended nothing had happened. Pretended Alfie had locked the car and was making his way up the garden path. Her collusion – which she denied with her walk and the tone of her words – was deeply seductive.

'Come in,' she said, leading me into the kitchen.

Harry, I said to myself, tell her you're already in.

'I'll tell you why I've come,' I blurted out. I told her about Alfie. I stood in the kitchen hoping that she would turn to face me directly instead of presenting her profile at the counter.

She immediately went to get her coat. I offered to drive her to the hospital. She didn't ask me for details. She led the way to the car, produced a set of keys from her coat pocket, got into the driver's seat and started the engine. It was the car she had shared with Alfie before he had moved to the basement in Earls Court.

'He's going to be all right,' she said. I wasn't sure whether or not this was a question.

'Yes,' I said. 'He's going to be fine.'

'They're out to crucify him,' she said. 'You know that?'

'Yes. He told me.'

'Can you help him, Harry?'

'I'm doing my best.'

'I'm sure you are.'

Her unqualified appreciation left me abject. Now she wanted to know the circumstances of his attack. My response was purposefully vague. She saw through that. She steadily increased the speed at which she drove.

'You know what happened, don't you? Somebody tried to kill him.'

'I know.'

She was holding back tears.

'They poisoned him.'

'I know about that.'

'He is going to survive, isn't he? They haven't completely destroyed him, have they?'

'We're talking about Alfie here . . .'

She gave a little nervous laugh. 'Yes. Of course we are. Silly me.'

We were moving very fast but nonetheless she pulled out from behind five dusty builders in a battered white car and drove faster still. Evidently this kind of danger she could measure with infinitesimal accuracy. I could see Alfie put a ginger-root hand over his clapped-out heart, his purple face beaming with approval.

While Ruth was in the hospital making her unauthorised visit, I sat in the car with a bad taste in my mouth. I thought about Alfie's lousy life and what I might do to better his lot. There was the sting of hypocrisy in this, but I would have to get over that. My concern was genuine. Thinking about Alfie's lot got me thinking about Holland. I should have been watching Toby instead of staring at the hospital building across the street. I should have been thinking about Holland's daughter but instead I was thinking about his singing sentimental songs and his tie-rolling. Alfie hadn't told me the full story. I was sure of that, though what he was holding back was a mystery. I have seen my share of arch-manipulators and bullies. I recognise their kind instantly. I can see what they are doing as they do it. I was thinking about Holland turning his slow eyes on me and my registering something altogether more sinister. I decided I would have to pay him another visit. Get him to look at me again. Get him to sing me a song.

There was nothing I was doing of which my friend Alfie would have approved, but that was no longer an issue.

Part Two

CHAPTER 9

I was determined that I had put behind me my brief encounter with a friend's wife. I was free to contemplate the matter from a safe distance. That was my thinking as I made my way to Holland's West End office. I thought about the downwards-slanting smile that made her eyes sparkle. I had removed a speck of grit from the corner of one eye with the tip of my tongue when other methods had failed. Did she remember that, I wondered?

The morning sunlight made the Minton tiled floor in the hallway of Holland's office deceptively inviting. It also showed up the hairline cracks that were concentrated in one small area. Somebody had dropped a safe doing a midnight flit, perhaps. There was an ancient wooden index board with its worn slats and sliding strips displaying company names painted in gold or black. It suggested a warren of gloomy offices with a transitory population. Transitory, that is, except for Holland's company. He had a brass plaque fixed above the index board. He probably held a ninety-nine-year lease on the entire building.

I climbed the staircase, a robust 1930s replacement for the original. I was greeted on the second floor by Holland's secretary. She had an embalmer's touch with make-up. She had a twittery voice that suggested she could stay afloat on an upturned umbrella. I knew not to get smart with her.

'An appointment?' No. I did not. I told Ms Twitter that I had an open line of sorts. I tried not to sound intense and mysterious, but I observed my hands making small meaningless gestures. In the car on the way to the hospital I had got hard just glancing at Ruth's lap. I could admit to that now – even revel in the moment privately. It was something I could take away with me. That kind of taking was permissible. I had been thinking about Ruth's lap, climbing the staircase. That explained my restless hands.

'Mr Holland is in a meeting.'

'I can wait.'

'He's liable to be some time.'

'I'll just sit here until he's free. I won't take much of his time.'

'It's in connection with?'

'His daughter.'

'Ah. Please sit down.'

She rose to her feet promptly and I sat down. She entered an adjoining room. She barely opened the door. She seemed to slide sideways through a narrow crack. I speculated that Holland would have two doors to his office, the second providing for private access.

I had a quick look around me. There were no framed show posters, playbills or photographs of famous clients. The office furnishings were antique. Polished oak floor. Persian rugs. Small oil paintings of pastoral scenes. A large green glass bowl of fruit beside which was a stack of small china plates and silver knives. There was a film of dust over everything. The windows had been cleaned on the inside, but not the outside. They were set in walls covered with red damask. Did he have his staff clean their own space? I could see him cleaning the inside of the window panes himself with newspaper. I could see him standing on his secretary's chair in another of his many pairs of Jermyn Street slippers.

I might call on Ruth again one day, I thought. Blow on the soles of her soft white feet. She would say nothing. She would carry on regardless.

From Holland's inner office came the sound of a second door shutting.

Powerful men, or men with delusions of power, understand that their minions strive to ensure that their master's life is uneventful. There are, of course, those little demonstrations devised to advance careers. That, too, is understood. But the master can get jealous of what he misses, or thinks he misses. He assumes that his judgement of character will light the way and ultimately will save him. It's a fair assumption, but he must never assume that his judgement in this respect is infallible.

Mr Holland had me summed up when we were first introduced in the restaurant. I was sure of that.

'Glad we could meet,' I said as soon as I was admitted. I gave him one of those firm, one-stroke handshakes.

You are? his look seemed to say. I'm not myself today.

How had Alfie described me to him, I wondered. A friend from the Yard? A chap from the Security Services? Something enticingly vague, no doubt. That was an approach a man like Holland would have applauded. Alfie had made a point of letting me know that he wasn't interested in what I was up to as a spook.

I was left standing while my employer made a show of arranging his papers. The inner office had lush, green walls. The ambient sound suggested that the room was lined with an acoustic deadener. There was more fruit. More plates and silver knives.

Alfie's boasts notwithstanding, Holland was clearly unhappy to see me. My first utterance was intended to dispel any fear he had that I was the bearer of bad tidings.

He pressed a button on his telephone, presumably barring incoming calls. With a palm turned to an empty chair he indicated that I should sit.

'Please,' he said, without addressing me by name. He didn't ask for information. If he was steeling himself against bad news I couldn't see it. What registered was his intense concentration. His starched display handkerchief pulled itself to full height in his breast pocket.

'Mr Holland, I'm a busy man,' I began. It was ham-fisted of me but undoubtedly perpetuated whatever myth my friend had sown.

He immediately wrong-footed me.

'You can't help us,' he said.

More ambiguity. Was there something wrong with me? I could no longer distinguish between question and statement.

'Perhaps we can,' I replied, conspicuously choosing my words.

'Well then,' he said, following up swiftly. 'I can ask no more.'

I followed in turn with another clumsy but effective lead. 'Alfie has tried to spare your feelings . . .'

He raised an eyebrow. No doubt he was thinking of Alfie's gut-wrenching directness in the restaurant.

'And you will not?'

'You want a result.'

'I understand. You have questions.' The same palm that had directed me to the chair again presented itself. 'Ask.'

First, I asked him about his son-in-law's family. General questions. Innocuous questions. Then, I asked about his relationship with his daughter.

'I'm a stranger, Mr Holland,' I said. 'You can tell me anything.' I pulled an indulgent expression which was meant to convey that I would cover any family strife with a piece of velvet.

'I have talked at length to Alfie. He is fully briefed.'

'We're lucky to have Alfie on this case,' I said. 'He's the best, but he's a sensitive being. He skimps on the detail to avoid distress. Now I've no doubt you told him everything we need to know.'

I left a silence for him to fill. The temperature dropped.

'My daughter hasn't committed suicide.'

'No.' Now it was my tone that was ambiguous.

'She hasn't run away.'

'I see.'

'I would know.'

'You would. And you would have told Alfie and Alfie would have told me.'

'The police have thoroughly investigated those possibilities.'

'I understand. And I'm sure they are still looking.'

'Please . . .' His head began to move as though his neck was giving out under its weight. The movement turned into a restricted nod. 'My son-in-law has what we want.'

'We're on the case, Mr Holland. We have him well covered.'

There was another brief, icy silence. His head was now rock steady. His eyes moved slowly about the room then fell again on me with a terrible weight.

'I cross the river every day. You think I wouldn't know if she was in the river?'

I squirmed in my chair. 'There are other –'

I didn't get to finish my sentence. He cut me short. 'I know what's out there,' he said. 'My daughter was not abducted.'

'Random attacks . . .'

He leant forwards, effortlessly parting the parade of bricks he marched back and forth on his desktop to keep people out. 'You find her,' he said. There was a little tremor in his steely voice. It made me feel low for having come to his office to scrutinise the man.

He pressed a button on his telephone. Our interview was at an end. He rose from his chair, moved sideways slowly, like a lazy tube train door. He caught me glancing at a framed photograph of a girl that was propped in a bookcase.

'My granddaughter,' he said.

'Alfie tells me she's at boarding school.'

'You will observe her father visiting regularly. He spends Saturdays with her.'

I nodded.

'She knows her mother is missing and she wants to come down to stay, but I've warned against it.'

'Her father agrees?'

'Well of course he does.'

'It must be very distressing for the girl.' Now I was mimicking his tone, and taking his lead on avoiding names.

'I'm seeing to her care.'

'You are . . .'

'My son-in-law is glad of my assistance.'

'Of course he is.'

Resting on top of a complete set of *Spotlight* catalogues was a photograph album which lay open at a portrait of Adolf Hitler.

'Good photograph,' I said. 'You learn anything from looking at that?' Tact was out the window that day, and there was a bloody-mindedness that went with my mimicry.

Holland performed the slowest grin I have ever seen. It appeared to be fuelled by a weary disdain cut with a very small measure of indulgence.

'Hoffmann,' he said. 'You know his work?'

'No.'

'He had Hoffmann take these studies before the rallies. He wanted to get the posturing right.' He leafed through a section of the album, holding it out for me to see. 'Look at this for a sequence.'

I looked.

'You can see what they were at,' he continued.

'Yes. You can.'

'You can see the immense value in it.'

'It's all familiar.'

'The first man to use an aeroplane in a political campaign.' The disdain had faded away and in its place was a suppressed delight in a vision and in strategies. 'I show these photographs to my clients.'

'The rock stars as well as the politicians?'

'Certainly.'

The telephone rang. He returned to his desk, taking his precious album with him. He lifted the receiver. 'Yes?'

He listened patiently. His patience seemed to make him grow progressively heavier. Eventually, he spoke. 'Billy, we are all under siege. Some of us turn it to our advantage. How many are there? . . . Trampling the garden? . . . Billy, now move away from the window . . . Let them. Everybody knows what's in the bin is only rubbish . . . Yes, I've seen the papers . . . Yes, I do know it's lies . . . It doesn't matter whether or not they know. Now you should know that. Billy, I want you to wear the same clothes every time you leave the house for the next week – precisely the same clothes . . . That way their photos start to look like library photos. You follow. Old hat. Yesterday's news . . . Yes, there is something else. Be patient. Have your mother call to the house if you think she can handle it. She's a lovely woman . . . And Billy . . . they're probably eavesdropping . . . Yes . . . no, it doesn't matter that they know our little plan . . .'

When he had finished with his celebrity client he put down the receiver gently and allowed himself a little sigh. 'New talent,' he confided. He hadn't lost any of the very small measure of indulgence in his voice, but it was a voice that was curiously reassuring. Dangerously reassuring. He closed the photograph album without looking at it. 'You'll want to get back to work,' he said and pressed another button. Ms Twitter opened the door behind me.

'Thank you for your time,' I said. 'I'm a lot happier.'

As I left the room he raised his chin as though he were expecting me to bow. I had a impulse to do it, but Ms Twitter's ten-foot-long arm had already reached around behind me to the doorknob.

I went back to watching Toby. While I watched I thought about Alfie and about Ruth. Thought about Ruth calling to the Earls Court flat.

She had come to thank me for helping Alfie. She said that she wanted to set things straight. She said that she didn't want to rekindle our affair.

Our affair – these words rattled me. What affair?

My anxiety, which manifested itself as vagueness, was readily accepted. We had put our encounter behind us. We were pretending that nothing at all had happened.

We stood for a moment looking at each other, then, we kissed. Now this would have to be put behind us. And all that followed.

I do not know how to celebrate. When there is cause for celebration I behave as if I should be in another place. I see this in myself and it makes me want to run. Ruth's arms around me were cause for celebration, whatever the cost. The rawness which I brought to our lovemaking was my attempt at celebrating. I think she understood. In any case, she responded in kind and I felt at ease.

When I returned to the hospital, Alfie's face had reverted to something like his natural pallor, but he was in a dark mood. His colleagues on the force had got word of his illness. Two of them had paid him a visit. When I came up in the lift they were about to leave. One was skinny and sallow; the other, fat, pink-faced and balding. I didn't want any introductions, and, I was sure, neither did Alfie. I held back in the corridor, then made my entrance when the two had departed.

'Friends?'

'You could say that.'

'I'll bet everybody was asking for you.'

'They tell me I've nothing to worry about from the inquiry.'

'That's good news.'

'I'm officially on sick leave.'

'There. You see. The organs of state looking after their own.'

Alfie's good name, his reputation and his pension rights were safe, he had been told. There had been no mention of the poisoning.

'What are you back here for?' he said, rounding on me suddenly. 'Have you found the body?'

His jolly, Reverend neighbour, who was standing at the television set with his fists in the pockets of his dressing gown, let out a snorty laugh. Alfie had spoken loudly, and now Jolly turned and took a step forwards as though he were about to burst into song. He was a man incapable of his own despair and so was drawn to the despair of others.

'What do *you* want?' Alfie barked.

He made another noise, this time closer to a snigger.

'Plenty of bodies downstairs,' he said. 'Hard to avoid them if you go looking, in this place.'

'Just sit down on your bed, Maurice,' Alfie said, his voice softening.

Jolly had a name and he liked Alfie using it. He sat down on his bed and turned to the television. 'It's not too loud, Alfie, is it?' he said over his shoulder.

'No, Maurice. It's not too loud.'

Alfie had decided that Maurice wasn't a confident pervert. He now had others under scrutiny. He beckoned me closer, pointed to an empty bed in the corner. 'That one there,' he said, curling his lip, 'I know him. Big slag-heap of a thug. I'm in here with villains and thugs.'

'They have to get well too, Alf. What's wrong with him, anyway?'

'Oh for GOD's sake, Harry . . .'

He moved to get out of his bed.

'What are you doing?'

'Something to show you.'

'You stay where you are.'

He was already out of the bed. He disconnected himself from his cardiograph monitor. That sent a message to the nurses' station, but Alfie didn't give a damn. 'Come and see this.'

He led me out of the ward and down the corridor to the landing where the lifts were located. The blood was rising in his cheeks. He was stiff in the legs but he forced the pace. In the mouth of the corridor he held me back by the arm so that we could observe inconspicuously. In front of a plate-glass window at the far end of the landing there were cheap office chairs around a coffee table. This was where the hardened smokers congregated. The area, however, had been temporarily appropriated for a thugs' family conference. That was the gist of the bulletin Alfie delivered in my ear.

'Fucking look at that,' he said.

'I'm looking. What has he got? Cancer?'

I took in the big slag-heap and his family.

'Every one a thug,' Alfie insisted. There were seven of them, including the sick father. 'There's more, you know. Uncles, aunts, cousins. Half of them banged up. Look at the gear. Look at the one with the gold necklace. He's worse than the father and what is he – twenty? See those narrow eyes. Born prematurely . . .'

It was a joy to watch Alfie read the faces. This kind of earnestness I could appreciate. He was eating peppermints again. I could smell them on his breath. He was pulling on his nose. He was getting better. He would be coming out of this completely unreformed. He would be back on his beat upholding the law and taking money until he was stopped, one way or another. He could never do enough for Ruth.

A nurse came looking for him. She dwarfed us both. We got him back to his bed where he ranted on for twenty minutes. When I couldn't take any more I looked at my clouded watch.

'I'm leaving now.'

'Leaving,' he exclaimed. He had seen through my flat, tolerant voice. 'Harry, you're getting too full of yourself. I used to be able to talk to you . . .'

'We talk,' I replied emphatically, though I could recall no instance where I had confided in Alfie my innermost thoughts.

'. . . And you'd be able to listen for a whole night.'

'I'm listening right now. It's just we have a job to do, remember?' This assertion was beginning to sound distinctly lame but that didn't seem to matter at the time. Perhaps they had Alfie on happy pills and they didn't agree with his system.

'Did you get photographs?'

'Yes.'

'Anything interesting?'

'No.'

'You've developed and printed them?'

'No.'

'Then how do you know?'

'I was looking through the viewfinder, Alfie. I know.'

'I believe you.'

'I'm relieved.'

'Print them up and show me anyway. There's gear in the bottom of the wardrobe.'

'You've told me.'

'Chemicals in the bathroom.'

'I know. I've seen them.'

'You better be looking after that car. I don't like the way you drive. Maybe we should have your old man to drive us.' He laughed.

Though he had heard none of our exchange, Maurice laughed with him.

CHAPTER 10

I was sprawled on the couch in that kip of a flat Alfie was calling our office; I was watching smoke rise from a dustbin across the street with the number twenty-seven painted on the side of it; I was thinking about the tiny fingers I had seen protruding from the letter-box of Number Twenty-Seven, wondering if they belonged to a child old enough to set fire to the contents of a dustbin, when the telephone rang up in the hall.

'Don't answer it,' Alfie called from the bathroom. It was a lame call, as though he fully expected me to ignore the ringing. He had signed himself out of the hospital against medical advice. He had summoned me to collect him. To hell with what Toby was up to. I was to get over to the hospital and park in the ambulance bay until he came out.

When I drove to the hospital I parked on yellow lines across the street from the main entrance. When he emerged into the daylight he was like a terrier springing out from a hole in a fence. He looked up and down the street and cursed me. I sounded the horn. As he approached through the traffic I could see that in spite of his terrier qualities the rictus in his facial muscles confirmed that he was still in shock. He became obsessed with examining his face in the bathroom mirror. He swayed back and forth, willing himself over the shock. When I spoke to him he seemed to be listening to the rhythm and the tone rather than to the words. It was as if he was trying to re-learn a code. Alfie's resilience was a complex thing.

I got up and answered the telephone.

'Yes . . . ?'

'Alfie?'

'No.'

'Harry . . .' There was a gentle downwards inflection in her voice. Relief or disappointment? I couldn't determine which.

'Ruth . . .' There was an involuntary hump in the middle of my utterance.

'Harry, I've been ringing all day. He never switches on his mobile phone. He gives me this number and then he doesn't answer. Will you get him to switch on his phone?'

'He won't listen to me.'

'How is he?'

'He's doing well. If he keeps away from the bottle . . .'

I was having selfish thoughts. I was hoping she would whisper that she wanted to see me, but she was far too discreet for that.

'I need to talk to him. It's important.'

I got Alfie to the phone.

'Talk to her, you fool. She wants to know how you are.'

'Never better,' he said darkly.

'You tell her.'

He wouldn't take the receiver. 'When this is over . . .' he began, but I cut him short.

'There's something else. Something important.' I

answered his anxious look with – 'How the hell do *I* know what it's about?'

The day Alfie had left – and I was sure now that he had left and had not been thrown out as he had told me – Ruth had got a call from a music management company offering her work on a West End musical. He had left to make amends; to put things right without involving Ruth. He couldn't bring himself to attend the opening night and now she was ringing to tell him that his parents were coming to see the show. She wanted him to come. She wanted to tell his parents about their son's heart attack. They knew nothing about it, and nothing about Alfie having split with her. Alfie swore her to silence on these matters. It had put her in an impossible position.

Alfie got very worked up over this. He put on a crumpled suit and we all went to the show. We sat with his parents. We gazed at that portion of Ruth which was visible above the orchestra pit's red velvet curtain.

Ruth, the cellist. Woman with long fingers and a perfect belly. Policeman's wife.

Alfie had made a late reservation in an expensive restaurant in the neighbourhood. It was an awkward business getting the five of us there. I was surprised at the frailty of Alfie's aged parents. Surprised, too, at his acceptance of that frailty. His gentle fussing. His concern for their physical comfort. The old man blew on the surface of his soup, then sipped from the bowl. Alfie didn't let that bother him. After the soup, his mother made a botched job of applying lipstick with the aid of a compact mirror. He just gave her an appreciative nod.

He told them what a good friend I was and they nodded gratefully at me. They were thankful for any assistance I could render their son, and they wanted to acknowledge what they saw as the exceptional bond between a childless couple and their unattached friend.

They knew nothing about their son's heart attack, or his split with his wife, but they did know about the poisoning. And they knew about the inquiry.

'It all has to be investigated,' Alfie told them, without elaborating as to what 'all' might involve. 'All these allegations have to be looked into, don't they, Harry?'

'Yes. They do.'

'Of course they do,' his father said.

'The truth will come out,' Alfie insisted with a terrible earnestness.

'It will, won't it.' Alfie's father had been a civil servant all his life. He had served in India, Gibraltar and London. Unlike my old man, his belief in the system was absolute.

'There's good people in charge,' Alfie blustered.

'You sit tight,' his father said. I could see the old man's spirit rallying. 'They know your worth, don't they, Ruth?'

'They know,' Alfie's mother echoed.

Ruth confirmed that they knew Alfie's worth.

A bright future was then predicted for Ruth with her cello.

'We're very proud of you,' Alfie's mother said, repeating herself yet again. And they were.

Alfie's father insisted on paying for the dinner. He put a twenty-pound note on the little silver tray without looking at the bill for dinner for five. Alfie covertly made up the difference. His father shook hands with the waiter before leaving. Alfie put his arm around the old man's shoulder to guide him out on to the street. Ruth walked with her mother-in-law. I trailed behind.

Alfie knew that I had killed a man in Chinatown. I shot him because he was beating somebody I cared about. It was just a little more than he deserved. Alfie thought it was 'business' because my controller, Hamilton, got me out of the fix. The circumstances of my release became one of those unconfirmed and unconfirmable stories policemen like to tell one another to paint themselves clean by comparison. It was a very short story of a man released on a nod. The story, I suspect, was quickly embellished with ludicrous detail.

Such stories are dangerous. I know, because an understrapper functions in a world of half-truths. Here was something else I was trying to put behind me.

'What are you doing?' Alfie demanded in a light voice that was sinister.

'What do you mean, what am I doing? I'm driving the car.'

'That thing you're doing . . . you were doing it when you drove us to the theatre . . .'

'What thing?'

'That thing with your head. The way you're looking at the road in front . . .'

'I'm driving your car, Alfie.'

'Your head isn't straight. You're looking crooked.'

'You want to drive?'

'No, I don't want to drive. I'm just making an observation.'

We were back trailing Toby Harquin's car. He was on his way into the West End.

'You don't like the way I'm driving your car?'

'If you weren't driving right I'd let you know. It's just you've got your head turned to one side – are you telling me you haven't noticed?'

'Am I driving crooked?'

'No.'

'Am I steering into oncoming traffic?'

'No.'

'You just don't like me driving your car.'

'I'm just saying you should get your eyes tested.'

I like driving. I've always liked driving. Owning the car isn't important to me. I drive the way I live. Cock-eyed. I talk to absent friends. The illusion of invulnerability is a great comfort to me. So too the constant readjustment – but with the head turned slightly to one side. Nothing weird in that. I like to rest the palm of my left hand on the edge of the passenger seat when I'm keeping a steady speed.

'You should relax,' I told him.

'What. I should go fishing?' he scoffed. 'You have that fishing thing wrong. Fishermen *are* relaxed. They don't go fishing to relax.'

'I was rowing a boat. I brought a rod because of the old man. The old man is the fisherman.'

We were right behind Toby. Whichever way my head was positioned, I was watching his eyes in his rear-view mirror.

'You look at the animals on the television,' Alfie

said, 'and you think you learn about how to live your life.'

'No I don't.'

'You look at the giraffe and you think you can see further.'

'No I don't.'

'You go fishing in a cardboard boat and you think you've got your priorities right.'

'I relax.'

'You spend too much time thinking about what you've seen through keyholes and now you have a squint.'

'I go fishing with the old man because he likes to talk.'

'Harry, you couldn't wait to ditch him. I was watching you.'

He was sucking a peppermint. It was knocking against his teeth. He was making the noise deliberately. It was a way of punctuating his little spurt of cruelty.

'You saw those animals in the hospital,' he said. 'You don't learn from their kind either.'

Alfie's idea of convalescing was to let me drive him in his precious car. Even that was proving too much.

'I've been waiting for you to tell me I'm a fool for signing myself out. I'm asking for trouble – right? I'll give myself another heart attack and die in agony.'

'No, I'm not going to say that. I don't need to.'

'But it's all right for you to talk to Holland behind my back?'

'I had a few questions.'

'Yes. I know. You think I haven't been talking to him?'

'He actually talked to you?'

'You ask *me* the questions.'

'He doesn't give much away, does he?'

'He's in publicity. What do you expect?'

'We're not looking for publicity. We're looking for his daughter.'

'He's a private man.'

'Oh really?'

'You're going to tell me you've met his kind before. Everybody you know is private, right?'

'I used to work for a man who had the fillings in his teeth checked for listening devices.'

'You ask *me* the questions, Harry.'

'I don't like him, Alf.'

'Yes. You've told me. Something wrong with the job? Something wrong with his money?'

'With his money – no. With the job . . .'

'Harry, obviously I've made a mistake bringing you in on this.'

'Yes. Probably.'

'I'm sure you have more interesting work to do.'

'I was on holiday. Remember?'

'As soon as I'm well enough you go back to your fishing.'

'You're going on permanent sick leave, remember.' I gave him a hard look and followed quickly with a mean little grimace. This stung him, but he needed a smack on the jaw. Only the rictus prevented his face from slackening into something that might be read as an expression.

'So what did you learn from Holland?'

'Hitler was the first one to use an aeroplane in a

political campaign. Whatever he told you about this case, it isn't enough.'

'Explain.'

'He didn't ask questions about the investigation – nothing about his daughter. Instead, he seethed with hatred for his son-in-law.'

'Is that it?'

'"You can't help us," he said at one point. Why did he say "You can't help *us*", Alfie?'

'I don't see what you're getting at.'

'He has it all sorted in his head. I don't like that. You have enough troubles of your own. You should ditch this case.'

'I can't.'

'You owe him?'

Harquin pulled into a multi-storey car park. We followed.

'Harry, you make a lousy copper . . . What are you doing?'

'I can't park here. There are no spaces. I have to go up. You get out on the next ramp.'

On the edge of Chinatown Toby passed through a narrow doorway and climbed a steep staircase. It looked like the sort of place you might go for a haircut. Alfie knew the premises. It was an afternoon drinking den and late-night cocktail bar. A neighbourhood ghost slipped a hand under my shirt and placed a cold hand on my heart. When Alfie said we were going in after Harquin I hesitated.

'It's time we showed our colours, Harry-boy. We're just getting old watching him.'

'At last. Some action.'

'Let's see if we can spook him.'

'You take it easy. You need a rest.'

'So let's have a drink.'

'You've had a heart attack.' We were already climbing the stairs.

'I'm taking my time.' He turned but kept climbing. 'Don't you like playing the bungling detective?'

'Get on with it.'

'Don't give me grief, Harry. I'm a sick man.'

'Get up the fucking stairs.'

We climbed to the first floor and entered the cramped bar.

'You're l-looking well, sir,' the barman said to Alfie and gave an affirmative jerk of the head. It occurred to me that the phrase 'after your ordeal' was implied. Alfie had the same understanding, judging by his weak smile. I was expecting one of his lubricating insults. He chose to mimic the barman's stammer.

'No I'm not, d-darling,' he growled. 'We'll s-sit there.'

'No table service, sir,' the barman replied with a rush of perfectly formed words.

'This place is going to the dogs,' Alfie muttered. He was in another of his radio plays. He ordered, and gathered up our drinks. 'To be refused service by that man is to know what it is to be treated like a gentleman,' he boomed, as we moved the short distances between the afternoon drinkers. 'I swear, at the end of a good night you'd call up here just to have Edward eject you – kip or no kip.'

The flesh-touts and the panderers among the company were conspicuous by their glances and their proprietorial airs. They smelt 'copper' but were indifferent. Alfie was in a reckless mood. I could see another binge in the making. Toby was nowhere to be seen. He was in a huddle in the room above, probably.

Alfie smiled graciously at two prostitutes who were lolling at the bar. He raised our two glasses to them before we had sat down. He swung around to me. 'Should have brought your old man here,' he declared loudly and swallowed much of his drink in one go. He had yet to hand me my glass.

'Certainly would have caught something,' I muttered.

We'd chosen a table where we could keep an eye on the landing beyond the open door.

'Relax,' Alfie boomed. 'Enjoy yourself.'

I had to suffer this carry-on. Had he collapsed on the floor with another heart attack, I would have finished him off.

A short time later the telephone rang behind the bar. Edward took the call and we got out table service. He brought us two fresh drinks. He put out two fancy beer mats and a small dish of olives.

'Compliments of M-Mr Harquin,' he said. He had a smile drawn on his face with a stick of charcoal.

'Accepted,' Alfie replied. He turned to me. For the first time since the latter stages of the last binge there was light in his eyes. The tension in his jaw was now expressive.

I gave an ironic nod at his drink. 'If you think I'm going to be your monkey . . .'

But he didn't hesitate. He picked up the second glass and drank.

Just then, there were footfalls on the stairs and we saw Toby with the two thugs we had seen him with previously pass the doorway. They were escorting a young woman down to the street. Toby didn't look our way and we didn't look at him directly.

We followed them out and watched them bundle her into the back seat of Toby's car. We followed them east across the city. Toby was driving. For the first part of the journey he gave an animated lecture to the woman, who sat between the two slouched thugs. I studied the rolling of Toby's head on his shoulders and his sudden left-handed gestures.

'What are you doing?' Alfie asked.

'Are you going to start that again?'

'You're too close.'

'Relax.'

'I *am* relaxed. Will you stop telling me to relax. Now drop back.'

'I thought we were showing our colours.'

'On his own, Harry. When he's on his own. Christ. I thought you people were good at this. I should be driving.'

'Have another peppermint.'

She wasn't getting a lift home. Beyond that, neither of us speculated as to where they might be taking her. We didn't know enough about Toby's firm as yet. I got Alfie to give me one of his loose peppermints. He made a point of not having another himself.

'I have to be careful what I eat. That's enough about what I should do.'

I was surprised that the presence of the two thugs made him nervous. I put it down to his preoccupation with his own mortality.

'Now look,' he barked, 'you're going to lose him.'

Alfie kept his arms tightly folded. Toby led us through the Blackwall Tunnel and pressed on some considerable distance to Plumstead Marshes in Thamesmead, where he parked in sight of Belmarsh prison on a road that led nowhere. She must have done something to thwart Toby Harquin's prospects to have merited a ride to such a place.

It's not difficult to beat a woman in the back seat of a car. As a rule, they're smaller than men, so there is more room to swing. The two thugs started after another of Toby's lectures. Holland's assertion that his son-in-law was a vicious bully and a wife-beater instantly gained credibility.

'What are you doing?' Alfie asked. Nothing sinister in his voice this time. Just alarm.

'Give me the gun.'

'What are you doing?'

'I'm going over there. What do you think I'm doing? Give me the gun.'

'Are you mad?'

'The gun.'

'Harry, she's a whore with a habit. She owes him.'

I reached over and pulled the gun from under his belt. 'You want me to go over there and just shake my fist?'

I was already walking towards the car. Alfie came after me.

'Give it to me,' he growled. 'I'll back you up.'

'You can shake your fist.'

'Christ, Harry . . .'

I released the safety catch.

I had no sense of occasion. I had shot a man in Chinatown to protect somebody I hardly knew. That didn't generate a sense of occasion, so this encounter wasn't about to do it.

I came at the car quickly from an oblique angle. It was what I judged to be a blind spot for the rear-view mirror. They would have had to have been on constant lookout for intruders to have spotted me and they were altogether too busy. I put the snout of the barrel to the front passenger window and fired. I pointed so that the bullet would not pass through flesh or bone but instead exit through the windscreen. It had the desired effect. The passenger window disintegrated completely. The windscreen shattered but remained in its frame. Now I didn't need one of these fuckers to open a door for me.

I had expected that the woman would be the toughest of the three on the back seat. I was mistaken. Alfie was wrong. She wasn't a prostitute. Hers was a soft face, blotchy with fear. Under the light coat she wore she was dressed like a student and she had pissed her jeans.

'Are you all right?' I asked in my best quiet voice.

I think she took me for a mad evangelist. In any case, she did not reply. Instead, she struck one of her escorts on the chin with a thrust of her elbow. In spite of her treatment she could not bring herself to put her body weight behind the blow.

'Very good,' I declared. I could hear Toby grinding

his teeth. His saliva had turned to foam from all his talking.

'Your identification, copper.' He held out his hand.

'I'm no copper,' I told him. 'You've all heard about the Guardian Angels . . . ?

'Fuck off,' said one of the thugs; the one with the sore chin. I smacked him on the bridge of his nose with the butt of the Centennial. He let off a little bat squeak. There was an involuntary squeak from the woman, too.

'My beret and my T-shirt are in the post.'

I think about such moments and I am embarrassed by my primitive behaviour. I feel the tomahawk slip from my sleeve and I catch it by the heel and I wield it with speed and efficiency. The tension isn't cultivated. The moment lacks ritual. It passes too quickly. The impulse carries more meaning than any ritual, but the lesson isn't learnt. A result is achieved, but there is a lack of appreciation from all parties concerned.

The instant I had discharged the shot Alfie had withdrawn to the middle of the greasy cement road. He was now performing a nervous dance. The small, concise gestures that I associated with those ginger-root hands had given way to movements that were part of the semaphore vocabulary of a drunk sailor.

'Everybody out.'

They all got out of the car. Alfie's dance was now restricted to the swaying motion I had seen him practise in front of the bathroom mirror.

'What's your name?' I asked the young woman.

'Claire.'

'Claire, you go to my partner there.'

She shook her head violently, but her neck muscles seemed to have locked, which meant that her head scarcely moved from side to side. She didn't want to get into another car with two men. I could understand that. I just wasn't sure what to do next.

'You come over here,' Alfie said, beckoning to her.

If there was any chance at all that she would have got into the other car, Alfie's beckoning her demolished that.

'This way, miss . . .' he barked, turning his hand in tight little circles.

She was trembling. Her eyes were fixed on the gun in my hand.

'All right,' I said, 'can you drive?'

She gave a demented nod, the same muscular restrictions severely limiting the movement of her head.

I turned sharply on Toby. 'Keys.'

Toby retrieved the keys. The incredulity that registered on his face was tempered only by the shock of the gunshot.

'No – this way, miss,' Alfie barked. He had his warrant card out and he was back at his dancing.

The windscreen was an opaque mess. I knocked out the shattered glass.

'You'll pay for this,' Toby assured me.

'Yeah-yeah . . . You,' I said to the thug with the bloody nose and the sore chin, 'take off your leather.'

I wrestled the jacket off him, emptied the pockets and gave it to the woman. 'It'll be windy without a windscreen.' I gave her the car keys. 'Are you sure you can drive right now?'

Another manic nod. She couldn't bring herself to speak.

She got into the car. I put a finger under Toby's nose, then turned it on the prison in the distance. 'You can tell them what happened. I'm sure they'll let you use the telephone.'

I started walking backwards. Then about-faced and caught Alfie by the elbow.

'Are you mad?' Now *he* was grinding his teeth.

'What do you want me to do? Drag her into your precious car? She doesn't like the look of you – okay?'

'Give me that gun. I can't believe you did what you just did.'

'No?' I gave him the gun. We were walking swiftly now. 'She's no prostitute.'

'So what was it about?'

'You think she was going to tell me? She was scared witless.'

'I'm the police, for Christ's sake.'

'Were you showing her your warrant card?'

'Yes, I was showing her my warrant card.'

'Fat lot of good that did.'

'I'm driving.'

'Fine.' I gave him the car keys. We heard a screech of tyres. The woman took off down the road swinging wildly from one side to the other, leaving Toby and his thugs standing on the spangled fragments of auto glass.

'Look at that,' said Alfie, 'she's going to kill somebody.'

'Call a real copper.'

Alfie must have approved of what I had done,

whatever my lack of finesse. He swung about, pointed the Centennial at the three men and they ducked. He was grinning without it showing when he engaged the safety catch.

CHAPTER 11

'I can't believe what you just did,' Alfie repeated. He was hunched over the steering wheel. It was a manic arrangement of the shoulders, as if he was protecting something delicate from me.

It was evening. We were on our way to the seven-a-side football match at the airport. He was deeply apprehensive and was doing a bad job of concealing it. It had nothing to do with playing football. We were going out there to meet a couple of monkeys he worked with on the force. They had been taking backhanders, too. They were part of Alfie's little empire, and now he was afraid they were going to blab to the inquiry to save themselves. They weren't troublemakers like Alfie. They were team players and consequently more likely to be protected.

'And I can't believe we're going to a football match in a lorry park.'

'I like to keep up. You know me, Harry. Anybody who's had a heart attack gets put in goal.'

'Oh well then . . .'

'You'll like these people. I might be able to get you a game, eventually.'

Alfie's bravado was wearing thin and he knew it.

'See, the problem with you, Harry, is you're not looking for the bigger picture on this job.'

'The bigger picture . . . ?'

'You want to help a friend, and that's a good and honourable thing; and you want the money, and so do I, but then you go and do something rash because you're bored.'

'Now *you're* giving lectures. Everybody is giving lectures.'

He gave me an account of his first lesson in looking for the bigger picture. He was a boy again on the school ship in Gibraltar.

'There was a time when none of the bulkhead doors on that ship would shut properly. They were using the lower decks for storing dry goods and the bulkheads needed to be watertight. Then, one day, this wiry little man from Belfast came to teach us English. He examined the doors, went to the headmaster and insisted that the weight on all the decks needed to be redistributed. A gang of squaddies was put to work and when they had finished every door shut snugly. There had been enough movement in the superstructure to restore joints to their original dimensions. The bigger picture, Harry. It was a revelation.'

'And now you're a copper.'

'Now I'm a copper.'

'Did you learn anything else from the Belfast man?'

'He only stayed two weeks.'

'You haven't told me what I'm missing.'

'Did I tell you – the second time I rang your old man looking for you he told me, "Whatever it is, Harold says no."'

'Yes-yes – and here I am.'

'Here you are. Helping an old pal.'

'Who doesn't listen and learn.'

'I like your old man. He's a lot like you.'

'I'll tell you about his lesson in presenting the big picture. After the war he was sent to Switzerland to trace money the Nazis had sunk under the pavements of Zurich. He was a clever young man with an appetite for wallowing in other people's dirty business. He likes the company of embezzlers and crooks. I'm sure he likes you, Alfie . . .'

'We all like each other . . .'

'He likes people like you because before the war he only knew the world through books.

'This hunt was the biggest job he would ever have. He spent a long time in Europe and he got results. The team he was part of traced millions belonging to Jews. It's the thing he is most proud of in his life. He presented their findings in London . . .'

'And?'

'And nothing happened.'

'There must have been some response.'

'They took the reports, thanked him, and gave him an administrative job winding down the Trading with the Enemy Department in the Public Records Office.'

'They never acted on his findings?'

'No. And now the Nazi hoard is in the news again and it has nothing to do with his work.'

'But – his reports?'

'He went to the Records Office recently to offer his assistance in processing his reports, but nobody could find them. How do you suppose that made him feel about the bigger picture?'

'Christ . . .'

'They've gone looking for them, of course . . .'

Alfie's hunch seemed more pronounced than ever.

'Alfie, I'm finished with this. You've said it yourself – I make a lousy copper, and now I'm bored.'

'I need you to stay with me on this. Please . . .'

'After this football match we'll go for a drink. I'll be leaving tomorrow. You can send me whatever money I have coming.'

'Please, Harry . . .'

'I have a couch. You can come and stay.'

'You saw what that man is like.'

Then, from the darkest depths something came up the dumb waiter in my head and shot out of my mouth –

'Alfie, are you saying you told Holland that we would get rid of his son-in-law?'

There was a brief silence between us. He came out of his hunched position, as though he had finally realised the futility of it as a disguise.

'Holland thinks what he thinks.'

There was another startling delivery from the pit –

'You told him *I* would kill Toby Harquin?'

'If we found that he was responsible for his daughter's death, I told him we would see that Toby got what he deserved.'

'We would kill him. You told Holland that *I* would kill him.'

'*We'd* see that there was a case against him.'

'What? Plant evidence?'

'We'd make sure he didn't get away with it.'

'No-no, Alfie. You told him I would get rid of Toby, didn't you? You told him I was the man for the job. All in a day's work for me. CHRIST. I can't believe this.'

'I didn't suggest anything about a killing.'

'Oh COME ON, Alfie. What do you take me for – a fool like yourself. Christ, I thought I was just an old pal holding your hand because some fucker spiked your drink. And what do I find – you have me pegged as an assassin.'

'You have it all wrong.'

'Do I. You put him up to it, didn't you? You told Holland his son-in-law was going to pay. How much are you really getting, Alf? Enough to buy back Ruth?'

His frustration had been building, and now it gave way to anger.

'There's no body, remember. We're looking for a missing person.'

'Are we? Well, you've changed your tune.'

'I'm not asking you to do anything to Toby Harquin.'

'I don't kill people, Alfie.'

'No?' he retorted. 'I remember a case . . .' He restrained himself and quickly reverted to a rational tone. 'She's dead. You and I know that, and we know who killed her. But we'll find her.'

'We'll get proof?'

'Yes, we'll get proof. One way or another.'

'Wait a minute – now what are you saying? Are you suggesting we sweat the bastard? You should have spoken up earlier. I could have blown off his ears. That might have loosened his tongue.'

'He's going to help us with our enquiries.'

'And then he gets killed – one way or another?' My

heavy irony didn't seem to penetrate. 'Toby Harquin gets killed?'

'We might talk about that, yes,' Alfie shouted, when he could no longer contain himself.

'We might talk . . .' Now I was shouting.

'Yes. If we find her.'

'If we find her . . .'

'Yes. And if anything has to be done, *I'll* do it. You don't worry.'

'I'm not. I'm not worrying. CHRIST – keep your eyes on the road.'

What a fool I had been to get involved. I ought to have known better. I should have left him waving on the lake shore. I had a flash of my being adrift in the rowing boat with Ruth's long legs between mine. My eyes travelling from her lap to her face and nothing visible beyond – I put that fantasy behind me instantly. ·

Alfie insisted that I was his McKenzie's Friend, as he put it; his personal adviser; his own, whispering saviour. He had a way of turning things about with remarkable dexterity – if he kept me straight, he would remain straight. If I knew my role, he would know his. It was a perverse declaration of friendship. He had let Holland think what he wanted to think. Holland was paying handsomely, and neither man would have had it any other way.

His McKenzie's Friend. Alfie's personal wars against villains and thugs and his other obsessions were to be shared only with a kindred spirit – actual or designated, it didn't seem to matter – shared with somebody who had crossed thresholds as he had done.

Share his obsessions – not the new Harry Fielding. The new Harry Fielding was disengaging. He was walking away from his sick copper friend and counting himself fortunate to have learnt about the bigger picture in time.

For the rest of the journey to the airport Alfie applied a fierce concentration to the road ahead. I thought back over my encounters with Sydney Holland. The strange formality. The awkwardness. The ill-fitting joints in the conversation. Put this one fact in place – that Holland thought he was addressing a righteous executioner – and it made perfect sense.

Holland wanted me to frighten him. He wanted to look into the face of vengeance. He was imagining the deed being undertaken with great efficiency. For all his tie-rolling he was a man who liked a radical solution.

Had Alfie put him up to it?

'This won't take long,' he said, breaking the silence. 'Whatever they tell me, I'll know if they're going to betray me.'

There was a hollow ring to his words. Betrayal seemed such a grand concept to apply to a couple of crooked coppers being frightened into telling the truth, and Alfie knew it.

'My couch is a hell of a lot more comfortable than that thing I'm sleeping on now,' I said as we turned off the motorway. My words also had a hollow ring. I was thinking about Ruth.

As we approached a service entrance in the airport perimeter fence, I realised that I had been thinking a lot about Ruth. I had secreted her among those absent friends to whom I talked as I drove. Driving Alfie's car that afternoon I had been talking to her. I had been flirting easily with her while Alfie squirmed in the front passenger seat criticising my driving and talking about giraffes.

The airport security man at the gate recognised Alfie at a glance and gave one of those deadpan nods that only bouncers and checkpoint-Charlies can perform convincingly. He waved us through, tapping his wristwatch in admonishment. Evidently we were late.

'New recruit,' Alfie shouted, indicating me as we passed. 'Forgot his kit.'

The vastness of the airport complex, the noise, the order and the harmonious movement all seemed to steady Alfie's nerve. He was sitting well back in the driver's seat now. He was taking time to glance at me when he spoke.

'Customs got this game going.'

'Really . . .' I replied tersely. I was trying not to let my thoughts bunch up; trying to think in absolute terms. I was trying to displace a cold rage with a cool sense of wonder at my being utterly misjudged. No such enlightenment was forthcoming, however.

'Smug bastards in Customs. Lousy footballers. They'd rather watch a game on television.'

'Must be something in their nature.'

'They've been bringing in other bastards from God knows where. And they can play. We're running a check. Our gang used to be a sorry sight, but not any more. We've brought in a couple of action men from Special Branch – overweight fuckers, but ruthless football machines. We've co-opted a fireman and a screw.'

He knew I wasn't listening, but he continued.

'I expect your gang up the river like to watch it on the box.'

'What?'

'Too busy protecting the realm to get out in the park.'

'I'm killing nobody, Alfie.'

'Look. They've started without me.'

There was still some light in the summer sky, but the security floodlights were lit. A large space between two banks of lorries was illuminated evenly. There were virtually no shadows. When the Berlin Wall came down the killing zone was dispatched to be stored in places like this.

There were proper seven-a-side goalposts with nets, and basic pitch markings over the parking grid. One team was dressed like cycle couriers. The other was dressed for a policemen's barbecue. Alfie undoubtedly played for the latter and, clearly, they were the under-dogs. Customs were not the sedentary oafs he had painted. Both sides were playing a hard, physical game. The coppers played with a fierce collective clumsi-ness.

I thought there might have been somebody from Air Traffic Control refereeing, but there was no referee. Not that night, anyway. There were a lot of clipped shouts and protests quickly stifled by the immediate demands of the next set piece or counter-attack.

There were no women present. There were several men watching from the sidelines; standing squarely, shoulder to shoulder, as though formally presenting their Masonic aprons for inspection. I picked out the one I thought might be Wally Preston, our head-banging friend. Wally, I was sure, was a seven-a-side man. Others were sitting in their cars with the doors open and their feet out on the tarmac. They were all dressed in their kit, ready for a game. There were no spectators. I felt I should have been wearing a ball and chain to explain my presence.

Our headlights swept into the play and immediately dissipated in the pool of light as we drew alongside an articulated lorry and parked.

'This won't take long,' Alfie repeated.

I didn't need convincing of that.

'We might have to wait until half-time.' Alfie had already opened his door to let in the game. 'Of course somebody in Customs might break open Tommy's head with one of those tackles. Then, I get to talk to him sooner.'

I recognised the monkey he was talking about. I had seen him before. He was one of the two colleagues who had visited Alfie in hospital. He was the heavy, pink-faced one with the monk's bald patch. The other hospital visitor was standing on the far sideline. Tommy was a self-appointed captain. He was doing most of the shouting. I watched Tommy. He was probably a nice man at home, but out here he needed a good kicking. If I was being charitable, I would have said that he was acting tough because he was afraid that he didn't belong; but that would have been a pathetic observation – and, besides, I wasn't feeling charitable. Furthermore, this man had

Alfie wringing his sweaty hands because of what he could do to him.

'Won't be long now.'

But nobody was about to bring Tommy down, and Alfie couldn't wait until half-time. He got out of the car and made his way to his other hospital visitor. Tommy caught sight of him in transit and gave him a big, friendly wave, but when he saw him talking to the other monkey he stopped the game – or rather, he left the pitch and the game stopped momentarily. Tommy's position, but not his captaincy, was quickly filled by somebody who got out of one of the cars.

Everybody would talk to the inquiry but nobody would co-operate. That had been the initial line. The tried and tested approach. From the posturing and the tight gestures I could see that this had been swept aside. I didn't need to hear what was being said to grasp that Alfie was to be sacrificed.

Nothing would happen, of course. I could see Tommy telling him that. Permanent sick leave. Good name and reputation intact. Pension assured. A heart attack could be a wonderful thing.

CHAPTER 12

'Right,' he said, getting back into the car, 'I know where I stand.'

No, he didn't.

'Now what?'

'Now I want to see somebody.'

'Who's that?'

'One of my choirboys – Boxer. I've told you about him. I was looking for him because he had something for me. He's rung in looking for me, they tell me.'

'Your friend there,' I said with a cursory nod, 'he's going to talk to the investigating officer, isn't he?'

'Yes, he's going to talk.'

'He told you straight to your face?'

'He asked my advice.'

I let out an incredulous laugh. 'He asked you – "What should I do, Alf?"'

'What should I do . . .'

'And you have no Mason's apron to protect you.'

'No apron.'

'You gave him your blessing?'

'I did not. I told him what I thought of him and the rest of them.'

'And what did he say to that?'

'He gave me my telephone messages.'

At that point the underdogs scored. Alfie turned the

key in the ignition, jammed the gear stick into reverse and dropped a heavy foot on the accelerator. We swung around in an arc.

'You know what makes me sick, Harry?'

'Don't tell me – there's others who are much worse. You're only in the ha'penny place.'

'I didn't go looking for the money. It was offered.'

'Oh, well then.'

We lurched forwards. He drove as though he expected to be airborne before reaching the gate in the perimeter fence.

'I took it, yes. Of course I took it . . .'

I was going to say – why 'of course'?, but I wasn't really interested in Alfie's sins any more.

'Look,' he said, 'maybe you *should* leave me to handle this myself.'

'Damn right.' My presence was fuelling his fantasy of controlling the events that were consuming him. I was getting out. I was going to ring about that job in the hotel.

'I always thought if somebody asked questions about this money we'd be accused of blackmail or extortion by our porn-king friends. That's what they do. They point the finger at us and they say we came to them with threats. They produce diaries with details recording every payment. The anti-corruption gang – they see through that. And if they choose not to see through it, the diaries can be beaten. Either way, there's no inquiry. It's different when one of your own points the finger. Then you know they're out for blood and they want something that looks like a purge.'

The security man waved us through. It was just as well, because Alfie wasn't about to stop.

I told him he should switch on his mobile phone. He just grunted.

'This Boxer – doesn't he have your mobile number?'

Another grunt.

'Ruth might need to ring you.'

'She has the number at our office.'

'No-no. Your flat. She has the number of the public telephone in the hall of that dump you now live in.'

'Whatever . . . she has our number.'

'Not *our* number. She doesn't need to talk to me. *Your* number.'

'All right. She's got my number.'

'What are you afraid of? It isn't as though you're asking her to kill somebody and you're afraid she'll say no.'

'Will you stop that talk. I'm trying to think.'

'Ruth will want to know about your partner talking to the inquiry. She'll want to know because she cares. Grow up, Alfie. She knows about everything else.'

'All right, all RIGHT.' He switched on his mobile.

To others he may have appeared to be a stubborn man fearlessly wrestling with his own needs, but I knew better. I knew that Ruth was a jewel on his tongue. He had decided that if he opened his mouth to give voice to his fears he would lose her for ever. Switching on his mobile phone constituted an enormous risk. I realised now how difficult the dinner with Ruth and his parents had been for him.

None of this, however, made me inclined to act as an assassin.

'Alfie, it doesn't matter how much Toby Harquin deserves it, or how much Sydney Holland is prepared to pay for the good deed. You have to walk away from this.'

'You have that all wrong.'

'No I don't.'

'What are you worrying about? You're leaving tomorrow.'

'I am.'

'I'm just taking Holland's money to find out what Toby has done with his daughter. You're the one who's been firing guns, Harry . . .'

To punctuate the point he gave a neat turn of the wrist that allowed him to cut me in two with an index finger. I glared at him. Gave a little angry nod, then turned away.

'Good job I was there to restrain you,' he said, as we came out of the slip road on to the motorway. His fear of betrayal had been borne out. The mordant glee that I associated with his listening to lies had found new expression.

We were on our way back to Soho to look for Boxer. Boxer often ate Salvation Army soup and slept in hostels, but he also frequented the bars and clubs of Soho. Dingy or *sui generis*; dingy and *sui generis* – there were no restrictions other than the generosity of his benefactor. His circumstances very much depended on who he attached himself to, Alfie explained. A lot of the villains and thugs liked the runt, so he got to ride on their coat tails. He continually boasted to Alfie that he was well connected in the underworld and was permanently in favour, if not always flush with cash. His readiness to resort to fist fights with bullies bizarrely earned him a reputation as a good judge of character among those same villains and thugs. It amused them to ask him what he thought of the people with whom they associated. Alfie must have slotted into that pantomime nicely.

'Tell me about Chinatown,' he said. 'When I heard you had killed somebody and that you were being held in Bow Street I thought there had been a mistake. How could a man like Harry Fielding get caught, whatever his motives?'

I said nothing. My eyes bounced along the horizon. It was a relatively short journey. We would spend a few hours on a fruitless trek, we would return to the flat and in the morning I would return to the airport to board a plane.

'I was at the identification parade, Harry. You couldn't see me, but I was there looking out for your interests. I go to visit you in your cell and what do I find — you've been spirited away in the night by two perfumed men in expensive suits. You shot that man in self-defence. That was to be the line, and I don't mind telling you I was relieved.'

In a short time I would be watching coconuts floating downriver.

'I've been wanting to ask you — it wasn't for the firm, was it?'

'I was on a mission to protect the innocent.'

'Don't be sarcastic. Don't cheapen what you did. You were protecting that Chinawoman.'

'Vietnamese.'

'Whatever. You were protecting her. And you were doing it again today. And now I understand why you got caught the last time. You were reckless. You took a chance you didn't need to take.'

He wasn't fooling me. He knew I was meticulous. However, he did not know how devious I could be. He didn't have the facts. I could never give him the bigger picture. 'You'll do better without me.'

'But you were right both times, Harry. Something needed to be done and you did something.'

'And I'm going home tomorrow.'

'You keep telling me that.'

We went to a coffee bar first. Alfie asked at the counter. Boxer hadn't been seen there for several days. Then, we went to a place with live jazz, chicken in a basket and cocktails that were never the same twice. The house wine was surprisingly good. Somebody must have made a mistake. Alfie asked around. Nobody had seen his choirboy. One nervous pixie said he was expected, but he just wanted to impress Alfie. We spent half an hour in the company of three petty gangsters and their extended party. They greeted Alfie with a lot of hand shaking and unnecessary introductions. I was introduced as a colleague. I wouldn't have been surprised had one of them handed me his card and said, 'You should give me a call.'

They drew Alfie into their ritual rehearsal of intimidation tactics. Alfie, they were sure, would appreciate the fun. Getting what was theirs – that was the agreed premiss from which to improvise. They all liked Alfie. They looked to him to assert the moral frame for getting what was theirs. Nobody cared that I was witness to this performance. I was being ignored. I was sure now that I would get the card and the invitation to call. My disinterest would only act as a spur. I marvelled at how clumsily these people operated. I put my feet up and drank their wine and listened to the quartet. I clapped. I even whistled. I was marking time.

We spent a further two hours going from one place to another. We returned to a brasserie that vaguely smelt of sweet, rotting fruit. Yet another place Boxer was expected. We talked to Horace, a shady solicitor turned shady landlord, who had the top of his right middle finger missing. He saw me glancing at the hand. He held it up, then placed the bottom of his glass on the tips of three digits to show that they were level. Alfie laughed cheerily at this demonstration, as did the landlord with the three level fingers.

Alfie liked villains to have a sense of humour. That is not to say that Alfie *liked* villains with a sense of humour.

The story was that the tip of the finger had been lost in a Glasgow casino. There were no details. Nobody dared to ask. I wasn't interested. I was tired and bored. Horace told Alfie that he was 'sorry for his trouble', as he put it.

He was playing with Alfie. He enjoyed patronising coppers. Alfie didn't mind. It was nothing more than a distraction. Our level-fingered friend had a young woman with him. A teenager dressed like a burglar. She laughed nervously at everything he said; and from what he had to say it was soon apparent that he was a fantasist who had never got over having the top of his finger chopped off in a Glasgow casino. He liked the young woman laughing. He stroked her cheek to reward her laughter. He was a dangerous man in a primitive sense. There was a pervasive sentimentality about him that suggested he would always meet violence with violence, and that he would do so instantly.

He kept going on about how sorry he was for Alfie's trouble. I watched Alfie attempt to milk him for information. I was reminded of Alfie's impressive manipulative skills. His attentiveness was more than generous and altogether transparent. The landlord was too self-absorbed to feel short-changed.

'There's scum everywhere,' Horace declared, addressing the remark to me. 'We have to look out for our own.' He was grinning solemnly now, and that was quite a feat. He was grinning, but his tone suggested that he wanted to finish a brawl he had started with somebody else.

He turned again to Alfie. 'You think Boxer knows who did this thing to you?' If he heard who it was that had poisoned Alfie's drink he would send Alfie a message.

I knew Alfie managed his informants well. He had never compromised any of them and he paid promptly. Since the poisoning none of them had made contact. They were all avoiding him. Boxer was the exception and we weren't going to raise him in what was left of the night. The landlord was one of Alfie's informants but I could see he wasn't about to tell Alfie anything. His patter was forced.

Was Alfie oblivious to this in his new state of grace?

When he made a move to order another bottle of red wine I knew it was time to go.

A short time later we were back on the street, watching a young man dance to a car alarm.

I leapt from the couch darting glances into the fifteen corners of the room. Alfie's mobile phone was ringing. I couldn't locate it. I looked at my watch. I couldn't read it. The white early-morning light hit the face at an oblique angle and turned the condensation into a bejewelled cloud.

'Alfie!'

Alfie shambled into the living room and dug the phone out of his coat pocket.

It was Boxer. I didn't want Boxer ringing before I had got up and got out. I had wanted to wake and resume my redemptive existence while Alfie slept on in his damp basement bed.

But I also wanted to see Ruth again.

Alfie arranged a rendezvous with Boxer.

'You drive,' he said.

'You want me to ring Holland? I'll ring Holland on your mobile. You act the innocent. Like you've done with me. You pretend that the only job you undertook was to look for his daughter, you've decided you're wasting his money so you're quitting.'

'Just drive, will you?'

'You don't need me to mind you.'

'All right. I'll drive. I'll give you a lift. Wherever you want to go. You want to go to the airport?'

'I'll get my things.'

'Fine. Do that.'

'Christ . . .'

I collected my things and flung them on the back seat. Alfie drove. He told me we would pick his man up at Blackfriars Bridge.

'What are you doing?' I said.

'What am I doing?'

'There's the bridge. You're in the wrong lane. Pull over.'

'I'll pull over. Don't you worry.'

We waited for some time before Boxer appeared. He knocked on the back passenger window. Alfie wanted to conduct the interview driving through the streets, but Boxer insisted we stay where we were. Several times he glanced at the entrance to the Underground.

I was expecting a hardy little runt with a quick, cheap smile. In the event, he struck me as being the nervy, sensitive type, quick with a knife or a blade, quicker still on his feet. He thrashed about on the back seat, pushing my things on to the floor. He sprawled himself fully. It was as if a big bird had climbed in behind us. The sudden, nervous movement of birds bothers me.

Alfie introduced me as a colleague. Boxer liked the formality of that. It made him snort. I didn't turn around. I grunted something about not keeping us parked on a clearway.

'You've been avoiding me,' Alfie said.

'I've been calling you. Popular man you must be,' came the reply in a south London accent.

'And where have you been?'

'People have been making threats.'

'That's never bothered you before . . . Who's been making threats? What kind of threats?'

'I'm in the bookies, right, and this guy, he opens his jacket and he shows me a shooter.'

'Who?'

'Never seen him before.' He gave a detailed description, but evidently it didn't click with Alfie.

'We'll look through the books. You haven't told me why you've been avoiding me.'

'This guy with the shooter, he tells me if I talk to you again he'll use it on me, he says. Thinks I'm a snitch.'

'You are. If he's going to put a bullet in you for talking to me, why are you talking to me now?'

'Because, Alfie, I want to tell you about Pauline . . .'

'Pauline? Who's Pauline?'

'You might think she had something to do with you getting done with the poison and that . . .'

'Is there anybody who doesn't know about my "being done"?'

'No. Nobody that doesn't know. Now – Pauline is my girl, right.' He seemed to change the subject. 'Remember that picture you showed me of the missing woman . . .'

'What about her?' Alfie interrupted.

'I've seen her.'

That made me turn my head.

'Where?' Alfie and I spoke simultaneously.

'Can I see your money?'

Alfie gave him some money.

'I seen her with her friend.'

'What friend? Where did you see them?'

The missing woman, Vanessa – her friend had a flat above a drinking club in Soho, he told us. He described the friend. Gave us the address. Told us when he had seen them. The friend was Claire, the woman Toby and his thugs had taken for a drive to Plumstead Marshes.

Alfie went pale but pumped him for details, then said angrily, 'This is useless to me.'

'Wait a minute, but you said . . .'

'This is old news.'

I saw the significance of the date of the sighting. If what he claimed was true, it meant that Vanessa was alive and, apparently, at liberty to visit a friend *after* the date we had assumed she had disappeared permanently.

'I tried contacting you,' Boxer protested. 'Bloody never answer your mobile, do you? I left messages on the other number you gave me. Didn't bother you though, did it? Didn't I talk to you?' he said, sticking his chin out at me. 'I talked to some queer. He just said you couldn't come to your desk.'

'You should have left a message saying what you had.'

'I ring to make an appointment. I don't ring to tell you what I know. If I tell you on the phone, I don't see the money.'

'You KNOW I pay,' Alfie shouted.

'That's because we always meet,' Boxer replied, his feathers unruffled.

Alfie swung around suddenly. 'Don't get smart with me, sonny,' he said in a low, chilling voice.

The young man sat up properly in the back seat and wound down the window. He gave a short, dry whistle. A blotchy-faced girl appeared at the entrance to the Underground. She seemed to roll around the end of the wall. The girl with eczema, I concluded. She didn't approach. She appeared to be stuck to the wall. Another bird creature. She presented herself momentarily, then disappeared.

'You see her,' he said. The girl slithered back into the station. 'Pauline. I sent her to tell you about the woman and she sees you getting done over with the poison. I should have gone to see you myself, I know, but I got a fright. So, I'm here now. She told me you were cursing at her when you were on the ground. She's the one that called the ambulance. So now you know she had nothing to do with you getting done and she called the ambulance.'

'So now I know. Get out. You've been no help at all.' Alfie's mind was racing. He had stopped listening. That's always a mistake.

'I have another little titbit,' said Boxer, one foot already out of the car. Foolishly, Alfie forked out another couple of notes.

'Nobody gives a shit about me talking to you now, Alfie. You're out of the game. That's the word.'

That was as much as Alfie got for his second greasing.

What this meant was that Vanessa Harquin was alive and hiding from her husband. The reason for Toby interrogating Vanessa's friend in the car was clear. He thought she might be able to tell him where his wife was hiding.

'Well, Alfie,' I said as we pulled away into the morning traffic, 'it appears you *are* looking for Holland's daughter after all.'

There was no reply.

Alfie had been poisoned. He had suffered a heart

attack. He was finished as a copper and he couldn't bear to face his wife. On the positive side, he had survived the poisoning and the heart attack and, as things stood, it wasn't necessary to arrange for his friend to kill Toby Harquin. Under the circumstances his silence was understandable.

'Toby is visiting his daughter at school today,' I said, 'but I wouldn't bother with him. If I were you I'd break the good news to Holland. Get him to buy you a celebratory dinner. Then, I'd show your warrant card to that woman again.'

'Harry, you could stay and see this through with me.'

'What – find Vanessa? No. You can do that.'

We were in the process of making strangers of ourselves, which was, of course, a futile gesture.

'Where do you want to go?' he asked. His breath was catching in his voice-box.

I was looking up at the sky. It seemed to be from another season and another time. It was a winter sky, and it belonged to one particular moment in my past that I could not immediately identify. It was icy blue above yellow clouds with pink and purple bellies.

'You can drop me at my old man's house.'

'All right.'

I was still looking at the morning sky. Alfie's voice seemed to be coming from inside an oxygen tent.

'You know where that is?'

'I do.'

'Coppers . . .' I muttered, wearily shaking my head. Alfie liked that.

Chapter 13

My father camps in his house in Muswell Hill. He has done so since the death of my mother twenty-six years ago. I admit, in recent times his camping has begun to look like a viable, if not desirable, existence to me.

Your father – he comes lumbering on to your doorstep in the end. That was what I was thinking as we drove north to Muswell Hill. Dead or alive, he sits down on your doorstep. He has come looking for something, but he will not say what.

'Turn left here,' I told Alfie.

'Yes. I know.'

He won't say what he is looking for, but the eyes speak – you're older now, they say. You're more like me. You can think of nothing to say to that, but perhaps you sit down beside him awkwardly.

I was putting this job – this sinister mercy mission – behind me. I was trying to concentrate on picking up where I had left off.

You're more like me, your old man says and you can think of nothing that might add to that. Then, he begins to mumble something that sounds like a recital of the alphabet, and you mutter something about things having worked out but you must be on your way.

'This one, right?'

'Yes.'

Alfie turned on to the quiet street where Cecil Fielding had his camping house. A house that had borne up remarkably well in spite of the neglect. A house that retained no ill will and was resistant to melancholia.

When we pulled in to the kerb my father was closing the hall door behind him. I was very surprised to see that he had a dog on a lead. Perhaps it belonged to neighbours and he was looking after it while they were away, I thought, but no. It was his. I could tell. It was an old dog. A red setter. Stiff, but still alert. I didn't know he kept a dog. The sight of it made me feel ashamed. I was more anxious then ever to re-establish a relationship with the old man. To sit with him and to listen, whatever sound he made.

The 1950s, when I was born, had been miserable for him. The fixed ideas of the civil service and the professions didn't suit him. According to my aunt Kate, he secretly fancied that he could provide a lavish lifestyle for my mother and myself by becoming a flamboyant chancer. I have no doubt he would have inspired a fierce loyalty among his attending scruff, but in reality he never was a practising chancer. Eventually he replaced his scruff with the park-bench medical exchange. Kate told me he had secretly revelled in the notion that he, my mother and I might live magnificently beyond our means on his eternally renewable resourcefulness as a discerning swindler, and that we would love him for it. With hindsight I realised that such a notion was at once his revenge for being ignored and an acknowledgement of his own best efforts having failed to make the world a better place.

He had expected my mother to outlive him. She was younger, and he'd boasted that she was more alive than any other person known to him. She had no need of doctors, except at the end. Even the natural order of things could not be relied upon. Somewhere, I speculated, there were old flames ever ready to take up with him, but they were never called.

He spotted us immediately.

Alfie gave him a big wave.

He advanced the short distance between the hall door and the garden gate. He stood between the gateposts, as a gesture of hospitality. He pulled himself up to his full height. His face became animated with a display of expectant tics. Somehow, he made the hedge on either side of the gate do something similar. The dog, too, seemed to know what was required. My father thinks I don't recognise that he is still heedful, still sharp-witted.

When I looked at him now, I had to acknowledge that he was scarcely any younger than Alfie's father, just a little more resilient. The years had seen the weight of his heavy head flatten his feet. Perhaps that accounted for his steady frame.

He replied to Alfie's wave with a slight downwards tilt of the head. It was as though we had been expected and had arrived late.

He had come a long way to the lake and had not complained. Nor had he complained when I'd left with Alfie. He had accepted that I was needed elsewhere, even if it was at the behest of my dangerous copper friend. I reminded myself that in my father's eyes Alfie was scruff and ultimately that made him a poor judge of his character.

Alfie was first out of the car.

'Hello, Cecil,' he boomed. He insisted on shaking the old man's free hand.

'Our touring fisherman friend.' This announcement appeared to be for the dog's benefit. He let Alfie do the hand work. 'You're not going to be sick, are you?'

Alfie laughed heartily. The animal grew restless. Alfie didn't like cats or dogs. He ignored it. I wanted to feign familiarity so I, too, ignored it.

'You're looking well,' I declared.

'Come to see me, eh?'

'Yes,' I replied, and felt foolish.

'Finished your business?' He addressed the question to both of us.

'We're in a work vortex,' Alfie said.

A what?

Even the old man was momentarily wrong-footed by this.

'There's no tea,' he said, 'and I don't drink coffee.'

'I'll get some tea,' I said. I reached into the back seat and took out my bag. Though there was no change in his demeanour, I could feel my father's eyes scrutinising my actions. Was this a gesture on my part? He didn't want any kind of a gesture. Or, did it signal that his son was in trouble? Was I running home with nothing more than the contents of a grip bag?

'You have milk, have you?' I said, buckling under the weight of his gaze.

'You're coming in?' he asked Alfie.

'You heard him,' I said before Alfie could answer, 'he's too busy.'

'Harry's right. I'm sorry I had to whisk him away from

your holiday, but he tells me you got the weather *and* the fish after we left.'

'Harold told you this?'

'He certainly did.'

'And the peace and quiet, of course . . .'

'You'll be wanting to get back to your vortex.'

'Yes. Thank you, Cecil. Another time, Harry,' he said, pulling on his nose, 'I'm going to give you a call.'

I shook my head to indicate that there would be no other time, but that didn't bother him. He got back into the car, swung it around on the road without looking for traffic and sped off in the direction from which we had come.

Cecil knew the dog was a big surprise to me. He told me he didn't sleep much and that he had got the animal so he could walk the streets in the small hours of the morning. He had had it for three years. It was mature when he found it at the dogs' home. He didn't tell me its name, nor did he speak to it or feed it in my presence. To introduce a third party would be to jinx their relationship.

'Your friend,' he said dryly. 'He's very enthusiastic for a policeman.'

'He is.'

'Always looking for trouble.'

'That's Alfie.'

'I see him commanding a party of policemen who spring out of a furniture removal van.'

'Something like that.'

The house smelt of bleach. There was a stillness encircling the old man, a zone he had created into which one had to step if one were to communicate with him. This house was the source of that stillness. The smell of bleach gave it a low-pitched hum.

I knew that he wanted to ask about my clandestine work with my trouble-seeking copper friend – how sordid a task had I been set? What price had been put on my rehabilitation?

'Are you back working with your friends?'

'Your friends' was his euphemism for MI5.

I raised my hand; gave an ambiguous shrug. With him I had always done something like that. I used to think he got a kick out of it, but now I saw in his eyes that this only confused him. He was disappointed that I would not confide in him.

'I see,' he said. 'Well, I'm glad to hear it. You should break with them completely if they're not treating you right.' He was worried now – what was I doing with Alfred?

I thought about telling him something approaching the truth. I thought about describing in detail, with specific examples, the ignominious existence of the understrapper, and then telling him that I had walked away from it. That I was a new man helping out an old friend and now that, too, was finished with. I would not tell him what I had done as an understrapper. Nor would I tell him what my old friend had lined up for me.

The new Harry Fielding was too indignant to speak up.

'But what do I know, eh?' Cecil said to the animal.

'Yes,' I replied with a confessional sigh, 'you're right. I should get out.'

I followed him into the kitchen. He made tea from

what was left in the corners of his tin tea caddy. The dog stared into its empty bowl. Whatever my father's knowledge of the work of an understrapper, he could understand that the attraction of a double life is the prospect of a life doubled; a chance to live twice in the one space and time. That is the theory, and that is the goal. The good understrapper is efficient and discreet. Nobody knows his business. The perfunctory work he does is meant to imitate small acts of God. It is a double life of sorts. A double life, however, must have been a curious aspiration to an old man who filled his nights walking a geriatric dog and his days sitting in the park with his cronies, watching the great social convoy.

'Good cup of tea,' I said.

'Of course it is,' he replied. Then, in a softer voice, he invited me to sit down with him at the table.

He interlocked his fingers loosely around his cup. He made a conscious effort to fix on me. I thought he might suddenly lose his concentration and say, 'And you are . . . ?' I felt I shouldn't move until it had registered beyond any doubt that, for now, there was more than himself and the dog occupying the house.

'I enjoyed my trip,' he said, with a strong measure of reassurance.

'Yes, I'm glad,' I replied with equal measure. 'So did I. It's a pity I had to leave.' I was repeating myself but we both ignored that.

'You should finish your holiday. You could rest here. Nobody will bother you.'

I nodded. I had been infected with some of Alfie's manic zeal.

I looked at the celery sticks standing in a pint glass of water on the kitchen counter behind him. I had grown up with an inexhaustible supply of celery sticks in a glass as the centrepiece of our table. Now, when the old man had forgotten to buy carrots, he would eat minced meat with celery.

'I just might do that, if you don't mind.'

'Do you want the newspaper?'

'Yes . . .'

'I'll get one, then . . .'

'Oh – I see. No, please. Don't bother. I thought you had it in the house.'

'I'll be getting the *Guardian* . . .'

He was sure now that he was not alone. He was already on his feet.

'I'll be back in an hour. Switch on the immersion. Have a bath.'

'Thanks, Cecil. I will.'

He was on his feet but he was taking his time leaving. He had to retrace the movements and reinstate the frame of mind that had got him to the gate just as we had arrived. He interrupted this process to return to the kitchen momentarily.

'By the way,' he said, 'I read an article in the newspaper about a police inquiry. Something about policemen taking bribes . . . or was it extortion . . . ?'

'And . . . ?'

'It was only two paragraphs . . .'

'What are you saying?'

'These people operate like diamond traders – there's no paperwork.'

'Who?'

'Crooked policemen. It didn't mention any by name, of course. The inquiry is ongoing.'

'What are you telling me?'

'It did mention the borough and the station.'

'And . . . ?'

'One officer suspended. Your friend's station house. I know that from when he rang looking for you. And from what you tell me, it's his beat. The thought just struck me . . .'

'Alfie,' I said, cutting in as invited, 'has just come out of the hospital.' I told him about Alfie's heart attack and temporarily resurrected my concern at his rash behaviour in what should have been a period of quiet convalescence. I didn't want any more talk about Alfie. This seemed a good way to conclude.

Cecil picked me up on my favourable report. 'His dedication to his work . . . ?'

'Yes. His dedication.' I knew Alfie's zeal by another name. What my father referred to as Alfie's dedication I saw as a double-edged ruthlessness. To illustrate my point, was he not doing to himself what the young woman in his story had done to the old man she married?

'Pushed him out, did they? The hospital. Another one of their experiments in the community.'

'He signed himself out.'

'Can't say I blame him.'

He turned and went on his way. There was a formality to his gait. He moved like a waiter wading through water. The dog modified its trot to accommodate this. Twice, he checked to see that he had the key to the door. He then presented himself to the hall mirror. That mirror had been purchased by his great-grandfather. It was a mirror to which all newborn Fieldings had been formally presented ever since. Generations of a thin lineage reflected in the same glass.

He had left the kitchen door open. He caught me watching him. He thought it best to linger rather than to bolt for the hall door. I gave him a nod and he was reassured.

'Don't hurry back on my account.'

He returned my nod, and left.

It's uncanny – sometimes something as simple as sinking into a hot bath is a perfect act.

I made it as hot as I could bear. It opened my pores and let out some of the rage I had suppressed. I lay motionless in the water and absorbed some of the stillness of the house while I thought about my bright future. The bathroom window was open. It was sunny outside, but there was a strong breeze. It carried the shouts of children, the barking of a dog and the crackling of a garden bonfire on a wavering ribbon of sound. There was the faint smell of burning paper.

Alfie, Sydney Holland, Toby Harquin and his thugs and the woman, Vanessa Harquin's friend – they all made a brief appearance as small, distorted figures reflected in the bath taps. It was therapeutic now to marvel at how Alfie had misjudged his old friend Harry.

'How do you like that . . . ?' I said aloud, drawing out the words.

I decided I would ring about the hotel job. When I got back I would send my tarpaper suit to the cleaners. In a month I might stretch to buying a second-hand car from

Solly. Nothing special. It would just have to be reliable. I could be happy with that.

Happiness – you don't have to earn it. But it gets complicated after that. For instance, exercise can make some people happy. You can be happy for no apparent reason. Now that's complicated.

I thought about Ruth. I sank down further in the bath. I found that I was addressing my thoughts to her. She was sitting just out of view, sitting patiently with her cello between her legs, waiting for me to stop thinking about her so that she could do her work.

Ruth didn't have good dress sense. The clothes she wore didn't belong on her. They weren't dowdy, but they weren't sexy either. She was sexy in spite of the clothes. She treated her body as though she were not responsible for it. There was some perverse attraction in that.

'Come on, Harry,' did I hear her say?

What would my old man think of Alfred getting me to kill Toby Harquin? I could afford such idle speculation now that I was soaking in his bath. I could sit on his doorstep and drink his tea, then leave. I recalled him telling me about somebody named Chaka – 'a merciless Zulu chief who was assassinated by his treacherous brother, who was in turn assassinated by one of his ruthless chiefs. All this because their predecessor, Chief Gordongivana, who was the best of them, had got himself killed in battle.' My father liked to emphasise that a man could be defeated by circumstance and that a wise man accepted this and blamed no one. 'Gordongivana may not have been killed had the morning haze and the smoke from the camp not combined to make reconnaissance difficult.'

Cecil liked to take an oblique angle on events. I liked the way he turned stories back to front. They didn't spin, like Alfie's stories. They weren't prefabricated. They were bags of bones shaken out on to the ground.

Cecil didn't know anything about the man in Chinatown; nor about any of the desperate acts I had performed. There were bones I had seen that would never be found.

Harry, I heard Ruth say, you're not listening.

Was she playing? I couldn't hear the bow being drawn across the strings.

It's over with Alfie. *I'm* finished with him, too, the poor sod. We're in the clear, Harry. There's just you and me.

I didn't turn around. Instead, I closed my eyes and concentrated on the sounds that were coming through the open bathroom window. I think she moved the cello from between her legs and leant forwards. I could feel her breath on my exposed shoulder. I started to hum, then I made a little whistling noise through my teeth.

'Alfie,' I said aloud. 'You stupid, stupid man.'

Some hours later Cecil returned with two of his companions, Kenneth and Reggie. He didn't want me thinking that he had no friends. He didn't want me feeling sorry for him. They were staying for tea, I was told. Between them they had brought six cans of Guinness and two bottles of sweet German wine. I gathered from my father's introduction that he had told them nothing about me. My presence was as much a surprise to them as the dog's had been to me. What had Reggie done to avoid being called Reginald?

They made what Cecil would have deemed a noisy entrance. I was invited into the kitchen with them and Cecil cooked us all a mixed grill. I made a pot of tea. When I withdrew from their company Cecil was lecturing his companions about criminals using stolen art treasures to launder money or as collateral. Now was the time for stolen art treasures from the war to surface, he insisted. The sons and daughters and nephews and nieces of the thieves were touring America with their catalogues of dubious provenances, looking for a good price.

Kenneth and Reggie were happy to be lectured by Cecil on the subject. They encouraged him and they were genuinely appalled.

When I came down the creaking staircase again the smell of cooking still lingered in the hall, but Reggie and Kenneth had gone. By this time the theatres had also emptied out, and the idea that my old pal Alfie had tried to dupe me might have seemed absurd had I not known it to be fact.

'I can give you something to sleep,' Cecil said. He was in the living room watching television.

'No, thanks. I'm fine.'

He saw that I was wearing my coat.

'Right then . . . you can let yourself in.'

'Well . . .'

'You'll want the spare key,' he quickly rejoined.

'Yes. I'm such a fool for forgetting to bring mine . . .'

He got up and moved to the mantelpiece. My gaze fell on the framed photograph of my mother and her sister, Kate, in their swimsuits on the beach in 1956. There were jumping in the air, delighting in their outrageous behaviour which was scandalising my father,

185

the one taking the photograph. He had captured the most evocative moment; the moment he was most shocked he released the shutter. In the oval mirror which hung on the chimney-breast he saw me looking at his handiwork. His secret admiration was evident now as then.

'You see your aunt?'

'Yes. I saw her about a month ago.'

'And how is she?'

'She's remarkably well.'

'Still carrying on?'

'You know Aunt Kate.'

'Indeed I do. It's disgusting at her age.'

He had disapproved of her promiscuous ways as a young woman and thought them an unbearable spectacle in an older woman. But he was grateful for her immoderate influence on his young wife. He may even have loved her, too.

'She was asking for you.'

'Huh.'

'You should make contact with her again.'

'She still has you changing her curtains for the winter?'

'Yes.'

'Watch yourself round there, son. Does she talk about me?'

'She does.'

'Ignore whatever she tells you. Does she still call me Job's Comforter?'

'She does.'

'And she calls herself a Quaker.'

'She says she's going to visit you.'

'Tell that bloody Irishwoman to keep her distance.'

He gave me a key which he took from behind the clock on the mantelpiece. 'You keep that.'

'I will.'

'Good programme, this . . .' he said, indicating the television.

I patted his shoulder. He went back to his chair.

I looked in the hall mirror, then I went to the house with the porcelain swan.

Part Three

CHAPTER 14

Three days later my plane dropped out of a leaden sky and made an emergency handbrake stop on the runway in order to stay on the dark side of dawn. The weather in my adoptive city had changed drastically. There had been a recent downpour, and there was more to come. For now, there was a fresh, earthy interlude.

I rubbed my forehead with the heel of my palm. I pressed it hard against my skull and moved it with a slow, circular motion. Once again, my life had contracted. I heard a faint cheer.

Embracing Ruth had made me feel properly damned. Damned completely. I wondered whether or not she felt the same. We had almost succeeded in turning an assignation into an affair. If it had been as much a revelation to her as it had been to me she did not show it. Had I stayed she would have tried to establish a routine for us. She would have tried to make ordinary that which was extraordinary, in spite of her knowing that I would leave in any case.

I was weary of my perceptions. Tired of the inside of my own head. Had I told her as much before leaving she would have ignored me.

The car I had borrowed from Solly, the one my father had said was unreliable, started at the first attempt, despite having lain idle in the airport car park for some time.

Never trust a man who doesn't have a watch.

The car was long overdue. Solly would be jumping up and down in his brown suit. I could show him my clouded watch. I could tell him that I liked this model so much I was prepared to buy it.

I wasn't in a position to bargain, given that I was coming back so late from my extended test drive. Under the circumstances, Solly would take it as an insult. I would have to give him whatever he asked. He might let me promise the amount and give him less. He would call me a tight bastard no matter what I paid.

Solly, I would say, thank God you're not like me.

I like Solly. He's a good man.

It was already daylight by the time I eased the car out of its parking space. I looked up through the windscreen at the heavy sky. Now that there was light reflected from the ground it seemed loftier; it appeared to be carrying more blue ink. Cecil might have painted it thus in one of his Christmas card scenes. There was nothing to read in it but the weather forecast, and that was a relief.

At that time of the morning the traffic was still light. I kept a steady speed moving across the city. The traffic lights co-operated on what appeared to be a concessionary basis.

I passed under a low railway bridge that was dripping rainwater. A slow-moving ammonia train rolled overhead making a nice, even rumble-click-rumble as each of the six reinforced cylinder carriages passed. I had glimpsed it earlier as it moved through the city on a raised loop of track. The lamp on the water-carrier on the end of the train made a crimson smear in my rear-view mirror before sliding from view.

There were two men on the steps of the maternity hospital. Smoke from their cigarettes curled in the damp air. They watched me pass. I yielded to an impulse to wave. Both men waved back.

Hotel work notwithstanding, my passage through the city seemed to affirm that I had a future. I had heard the sweet sounds of a summer morning from a bathroom. I had looked again into the Fielding family mirror and had seen that redemption was at hand. I knew it, though others failed to recognise it. Harry would settle for that. He was telling Ruth as much. He was imagining her lap in the seat beside him.

Solly was standing in the lane when I turned the corner. When he saw me approaching in his car he hitched his knuckles on to his waist and brought his elbows forwards. I waved and gave him a big smile through the windscreen. He didn't move out of the way, so I stopped and wound down the window. The situation required delicate judgement. I had the distinct impression he had been standing there for days, allowing nothing to pass.

'Back with a full tank, Solly,' I said cheerily.

He looked at me as though I were returning one used head.

'Solly – what can I say – I'm sorry about the delay. You got my message,' I said. It was a mitigating statement, not a question. No, he told me, he had got no message. 'I *did* leave a message explaining . . .'

'Pardon?'

I knew when he said 'Pardon?' in a quiet, reasonable voice I was in trouble.

'I'm sorry, Solly . . . about the delay.'

'Delay . . . ? Are you trying to ruin me, are you?'

'I like this car.'

'You like the car. Oh – in that case . . .'

'I like it so much I'm going to buy it.'

He let out a little shriek of derision.

'Cash,' I said.

'I had the law round here. The owner of that didn't like it when I told him his car was away on holidays.'

I knew Solly had bought the car, but I couldn't say as much. I had taken advantage of his generosity.

'That's terrible, Solly. I'm prepared to pay for it right now.'

'I got no message.'

'I was called away. I had a friend in trouble.'

He finally moved.

'Open the back door, ya bollix.'

I opened the door and he got in. When I said that I had been helping a friend in trouble Solly's attitude had changed significantly, but he felt obliged to continue with his rebuke.

'Right,' he said, 'eleven hundred, cash.'

It was worth eleven hundred – just.

'I'll have to go to the bank.'

'Not in this man's car, you can't.'

'Of course not.'

Solly reached around and stripped me of my protective sticker.

'Solly, I'm really sorry if I put you in a spot.'

'Are you? And still you didn't ring. Make that eleven-fifty.'

I got him the money. When I brought it to him he had calmed down. I gave him the cash and he made two mugs of tea. We sat in his pokey office looking out into his yard. Finally, he spoke –

'You got your friend sorted?' he enquired gruffly.

'Yes. I did.'

He grunted.

'That's due for a service,' he said, indicating the car I had just bought. 'Didn't get to do it before it disappeared.'

'It's running smoothly,' I said.

'Get it done by the end of the month. She's not firing the best.'

I think he was saying that at the end of the month I would be taken back into the fold. His children had already given it a rough clean with the kitchen brush. He took the eleven hundred and fifty pounds, but when I got into the car to drive away I found fifty pounds stuffed in the ashtray on the dashboard.

I parked on a street adjacent to my own. I bought a newspaper and a litre of milk in the corner shop. I spotted my Italian neighbour shambling along the wet pavement.

'Hey, Uberto . . .'

He stopped close to me, gave my hand a short, secretive tug. He spoke down on to his chest.

'Harry,' he said, as though he had summoned me, 'has he talked to you, our landlord? Our big boss man, eh? You have talked?'

'No. What about?'

'You get the letter?'

'Haven't seen any letter.'

'We're getting a letter. He's putting us on the street.'

'Is he, now?'

'I've talked. He tried to be very nice – you know . . .' He pulled the best supercilious smile I have yet seen. 'He wants the house for a dental practice.'

'A dental practice . . . ?'

'The dentist wants the whole house. A lot of money in teeth, Harry.'

'This dentist, did he call to the house?'

'Dentist – I don't know . . .'

'Or maybe an estate agent . . . ?'

'Somebody calls with the landlord,' he said, nodding.

'To look around? They knocked on your door, right?'

'Yes. They take a quick look. At first I think they're going to fix the place up. You know – paint the walls and raise the rent.'

'And my flat? Did you see them look in there?'

'I do not think they – maybe they look. But no. Not without your permission? Bastard. You think they look without your permission?'

'What did this other man look like?'

Uberto shrugged. He described a man of slight build in a suit and tie. Light complexion. Clean-shaven.

Did he have an accent?

Nothing distinctive.

Expensive suit?

Uberto gestured dismissively. He wasn't impressed with the suit.

'Nice continental cut . . .' I said to draw him on.

He wiped my words out of the air with a languorous wave of his hand, 'No-no,' he said, trying hard to be patient with me. 'Expensive shoes,' he added as a concession. 'Brown . . . English . . . with the little holes . . .'

'Happy chap, was he? Smiled a lot?'

Another dismissive gesture.

'Christ, you can't go away for a couple of days fishing . . .' I said, covering my concern. 'When does he want us out?'

'Two months – he wants to be nice man.' The same withering smile.

'And upstairs?'

'She's moving out next week.'

'Next week?'

'She's already found another place. I think he tells her first, as a favour. Dirty bastard.'

'Two months . . .'

'Two.'

'How do you like that . . . ?'

'Yes – how?'

He put a hand up in the air and kept it there as he went on his way, shaking his head in disgust.

'See you, Harry.'

'See you.'

From my window, where a patient might sit were he

in a dentist's chair, I looked across at the new rectangle of sky. The transparent rooms that had hung there in spite of the wind had finally been washed down the street drains.

Had my visit to London alerted some old enemies? Had I been visited by one of the chaps from the firm? Chaps are on the official payroll. They get a pension. They do dirty work, but are afforded cover and are never regarded as criminals. Vicious public school twits in expensive suits and car coats. All of them named George.

I opened the window and carefully scanned the street. Then, I turned slowly to take in my room. Again, I looked down into the street. An old man passing on a black bicycle glanced in my direction. He gave a twitch of his head in acknowledgement.

'Hoy,' I shouted, and pointed to the squashed card-board box of tomatoes he had lashed to the back carrier. The box was hanging precariously to one side.

He happily dismissed my concern with a wave and 'Oh aye' before he turned the corner.

I had left London abruptly the last time, and with good reason. Somebody from the firm had disappeared and they wanted to ask me questions. I had nothing to say about the matter. I could only tell them that the absentee deserved our contempt, and nobody wanted to hear that. Friends and acquaintances were forbidden to disappear – voluntarily or otherwise – without a wave of the firm's magic wand. Disaffection had to be sanctioned. There could be no sponsoring of a mystery that was not of their making.

I decided to suppress my anxiety. It would do

no good to have it show if there was somebody watching.

I stood for a long time pulling faces. I listened for the dull rumble of clouds and the boasting of journalists and policemen.

Then, I watered the plants.

Then, I lifted the telephone.

The hotel job had been taken. I was relieved. I had some money put aside. I would continue to live off that. I could live relatively comfortably for a while yet on the personal pension fund that my cautious nature had demanded as an integral part of any 'goodbye plan'. Cheap socks and budget toothpaste bothered me less than it would bother Alfie once Holland stopped paying out.

I had a fresh carton of milk and the newspaper, but there was no coffee left in the tin. I didn't take my jacket. I cut through to the park. I felt privileged in my shirt sleeves.

There were people playing tennis over the raggedy nets on the public courts. None of them was dressed in whites. The fence had all kinds of unlikely bulges – people regularly misjudged the trajectory of the ball and flung themselves into the wire mesh with tremendous force. If there were people who listened to the water flowing under the streets, there were people who straightened fences. Perhaps I could get a job doing that.

I had a stiff coffee and read the newspaper in a cafeteria on the far side of the park. I sat at the back so that I had a good view of the door and the street beyond.

In the evening I took a long walk by the river. It had grown chilly but I kept walking in my shirt sleeves. I tried to preserve that sense of privilege I had felt before; to make a ritual of my progress as my father would. I was determined to enjoy once again the small accommodations of a modest existence.

I slouched on the wall to watch grass cuttings float downriver. I tried to put Alfie from my mind, but I could only banish him to his secret allotment and I wasn't comfortable with this rosy picture of my friend Alf. Only thoughts of Ruth could eclipse the picture of her husband digging in the dirt.

I took my time walking back up my street. Everything seemed normal. It was only when I was putting the key into the hall door that I sensed I was being watched.

I went upstairs to my flat, switched on several lights, shuffled about in plain view, then ran the bath. The cold water from the cold tap mixed with the cold water from the hot tap. While the water filled the bath I checked the back lane from the dark landing window.

From the operator's cabin on the crane tower I had a commanding view of the entire street. A fresh breeze was blowing in from the sea and pushing the clouds beyond the mountains. There was a soft whistling noise coming from under the warped frame of the observation window. The cabin swayed. It was barely perceptible, but the movement made me distinctly aware of my own patience.

I remained in the crane tower for the best part of an hour observing movements on the street and in and out of the buildings. I studied the interiors of parked cars. I stared into the shadows. I could see no suspicious figure.

The telephone rang just before 2.00 a.m. I lurched out of bed.

'Harry . . .'

I said nothing.

'I'm glad I caught you . . .'

'It's two in the morning.'

'I thought you might be working. Or on one of your expeditions.'

'Good night, Alfie.'

'No – wait. I'm not looking for anything. I just thought you might like to know what's happened.'

'No.'

It was the same approach as last time. I could see him standing on the lake shore waving at me. Scruff in trouble. My father had yielded and given him my telephone number, after all.

'I feel a whole lot better now, Harry. I want you to know that. I've made a full recovery.'

He wasn't quite drunk. One more drink would do it.

'Well, that's something, isn't it.'

'They've given me a date to appear in front of the inquiry.'

'How are you going to handle it?'

'I'm going to tell the truth. What do you think of that?'

'Getting reckless, eh?'

'Setting a good example to the monkeys.'

I grunted.

'Get some sleep.'

'There's the other thing, of course . . .'

I said nothing. I steeled myself.

'What sort of a place do you have there?'

'You wouldn't like it. It's above ground.'

'Have you got a decent couch?'

I looked at the couch, a big shabby thing.

'Good enough for you.'

'That's not good enough.' He gave a wheezy laugh. 'Thing is . . .' He paused, then he abruptly changed direction. 'Is that offer still open?'

I said that it was, but I hesitated. I drew a breath.

'Have you got company?'

'None of your business.'

I could see it coming – another one of his lubricating remarks.

'You don't . . . ?'

'Alfie, get to the point. When are you coming?'

'Is there something wrong with you, Harry? You can tell me. I've seen it all and I don't give a damn. I said to Ruth there might be something wrong with you . . .'

'You did . . . ?'

'Some sexual ambiguity maybe, she wondered.'

'Did she . . . ?'

'I gave you the benefit of the doubt.'

'Thanks, sweetie.'

'I told her you weren't bent.'

'Not that you would mind . . .'

'Thing is, I haven't found Holland's daughter . . .'

'I wasn't going to ask.'

I *did* want to know, but I seemed to remember telling

Alfie some time ago that I was finished with London; that I was a free man.

'You'll be glad to hear that Toby got his car back.'

'Oh good.'

'I went looking for Vanessa's friend – that woman in the car – the one you frightened with my gun . . . remember?'

'I meant to say – fat lot of good you were on that occasion.'

'I haven't caught up with her yet. She went straight to her flat and packed her bags. But I *did* get to talk again to Pauline – remember Pauline?'

'Boxer's girlfriend.'

'She told me that Boxer was in a terrible fight and got badly beaten.'

'I hope you're writing all this down – I mean . . . now that you're a one-man police force.'

'Boxer was telling us lies, Harry. He happened to know Holland's daughter and this woman were friends – he'd seen them together a long time back. No . . . Boxer was just taking me for what he could get before I'm out on my ear.'

He had nothing that wasn't already known, other than the fact that Boxer had lied about when he had seen Holland's daughter, and that the runt had been beaten by persons unknown, probably for associating with Alfie.

Everybody was out to damage Alfie. He had been aware of that since he had swallowed the concoction at the bar. Being stung for a few pounds by his champion choirboy had hit him hard. But was he really taking up the Vanessa Harquin case? In his drunken haze was he now denying the true purpose of our stalking her husband?

'Tell your colleagues. Tell Holland. You don't need to tell me.'

He made a sucking noise with his mouth, as though half his face had been numbed by novocaine.

'Harry,' he said, 'you should have been here in my flat. I've had a visit from Toby and his friends . . .'

At that point I heard him suppress a tortured sigh.

'. . . you said you'd look out for me . . .'

'Christ, Alfie . . .'

'I'm all right. I'm all right . . .' his voice trailed off, then came booming back. 'Toby seemed to think I was trying to interfere with his investigations.'

He gave a short, jagged laugh.

Again, I told him to quit. His McKenzie's Friend was advising that he give his notebook to somebody on the football team.

'I shouldn't have rung,' he said, 'it's two o'clock in the morning. You need some sleep.'

The line went dead.

CHAPTER 15

The telephone rang several times early the following morning. I didn't answer it.

The park was virtually empty. I disturbed a wood-pigeon, which beat its wings in a chestnut tree but did not emerge from the foliage.

There was a klaxon wailing in my head. If I held my breath and starved it of air would it cease to wail? If I could silence it I would go to the races with Aunt Kate. I would hear the bookies shout the odds. I would stand on the terrace and hear myself shout home my horses.

'Alfie,' I said aloud, 'I know what you're at.'

It was lunchtime when I arrived at Kate's house to collect her. She lived alone in the family house, in what was once a Jewish neighbourhood. Standing between the living-room curtains which she had me change for the winter, but which she never drew, she had seen Jewish families long established in the street move out, bound for the suburbs or for other cities.

She sat me in front of a mountain of cold meats in the kitchen. There was a large quantity of bread, already buttered. I shouted up to her – was I to make sandwiches to eat now, or to pack for a picnic at the races?

'Suit yourself,' she called down. She had already eaten, she told me. She asked if I would fill the hip flask that was on the sideboard in the dining room.

She was upstairs getting ready. I suspected that she had an array of clothes spread on her bed together with several handbags and a roll of money. She would need to patrol up and down in front of the display before finally deciding what to wear and how much to bring.

Eventually, she appeared in the kitchen doorway in a flared maroon raincoat she had bought in the 1970s, an astrakhan hat and lumpy jewellery.

'Have you talked to your father lately?' she asked.

'Mmm,' I said. She had purposefully waited until I had my mouth full of food to ask. I swallowed. 'Yes . . .'

'And he talked back?' she said, raising her eyebrows in mock surprise.

'Yes. He's well and he was asking for you.'

'Has he shrunk any more?'

'I wasn't aware he was shrinking. When did you last see him?'

'I can't remember.' She was lying.

'He's still remarkably strong.' That, too, was a lie.

'I'm sure you could put him on your hand and blow him away. He isn't making a good job of being old, is he?' she speculated.

'As I say . . . still remarkably strong.'

'Oh, he likes his comfort. I know that. What I mean is – has he driven all his friends away – the ones that haven't departed, that is?'

'No. He's very good like that. He has a close-knit

group of friends. He has a dog, you know . . . a red setter.'

'A dog? I didn't know he liked dogs.'

'It's on its last legs. It was a stray.'

'What does he call it?'

'He told me it had a name that wasn't known to him,' I replied, drawing down my eyebrows, 'and rather than give it another name . . .'

She scoffed. I was reassured that she didn't know about the dog.

'Any of the friends women?'

'Eh – well, now that I think about it they're all men in the immediate circle.'

'Is he shacked up with a woman? You can tell me. I don't give a damn.'

'No.'

She reminded me that Cecil had what she called 'an unfortunate manner'. She would not elaborate. She was, however, prepared to concede that he also had 'a narrow charm'. This was meant to go some way towards explaining how her sister had come to marry him.

'He makes house calls?'

'Kate, I'm not the one to ask . . .'

'Of course you're not, love.'

'He asked me if you still called him Job's Comforter.'

'I hope you told him that I did.'

'I told him.'

The meat sandwiches were making me sick. I got up from the table, looked at my watch, and buttoned my jacket.

'Good,' she said. 'He's always been contrary, but I wouldn't wish him to be by himself completely. You say he's holding his own. There's no general loss of precision, is there?'

'General loss of precision . . . ?'

'He's not tripping over himself, is he?'

'Why don't you pick up the phone, Kate. Talk to him yourself. I'm sure he'd be delighted to hear from you.'

I piled the dishes with the meat and the buttered bread into the fridge.

Kate shook her head. 'He wouldn't talk to me. There'd be nothing said that was worthwhile, at any rate. I tell you what, though. I'm going to land on him one of these days.'

'Yes. You told me that before, and I've told him.'

'You have? And what did he say? Did he get the hump?'

'No. He said he'd like that.'

I was sure she would see through all my lies, but apparently not. I tried to usher her towards the hall door, but she stood her ground.

'I think he thinks he deserves me landing on top of him.'

I wanted to get going, but I was enjoying her banter. I felt connected. I grinned at her conceit.

'Is he still fighting his wars?' she asked, as she set about re-distributing the plates I had piled in the fridge.

'Yes.'

'Still writing in his diary?'

'Perhaps. I don't know.'

'I blame him for the way you've turned out.'

'The way *I've* turned out?'

'Look at you. A walking disaster when it comes to

women. You don't have to tell me. I know. Some James Bond, you are.'

She told me that my father was proud of my secret work, but that his pride in my work was more secret than my work.

How could I reply to this? I could only deny the legend which, of course, reassured her, and that would get back to Cecil to confirm his secret pride. I was heartily sick of my bogus reputation and cursed the day I had been indiscreet and confided in the old man. Why had I done that? To gain his approval hardly seemed reason enough. Perhaps I thought he could tell me something more about my enemy.

I thought about identifying the fault line that ran through her thinking, but I let it pass. Instead, I made a second attempt to get her out of the house.

'Are you seeing anybody now?' she asked, as we inched towards the hall door. 'I know a lovely young girl,' she continued without waiting for an answer. 'I know several.'

'I've been seeing someone. A friend's wife . . .'

'Not this fellow you're working with?'

'He's an old friend.'

'And there's something special about her,' she said in a gently mocking tone. 'She rides a motorbike . . .'

'Yes,' I replied emphatically, 'she's special. No – she doesn't ride a motorbike.'

She had locked the hall door behind us. We started walking to the car.

Not this fellow you're working with – I knew now that Cecil had been talking to her on the telephone. Worry had provoked the call, but I was heartened to learn that they were secretly in contact with each other. I was also alarmed at my association with Alfie being acknowledged, albeit by family, given that I thought Alfie was about to go through with Holland's bidding.

'There's nothing to worry about,' I said. 'It was a brief affair and now it's over.'

'*There* – you *see* . . . hopeless . . .'

She got into the front passenger seat and put on her seat belt without prompting. When I got in behind the wheel I looked at her. Her eyes were sparkling. There was nothing in them that spoke of hopelessness.

'Have you brought plenty of money?' I asked.

'I have not,' she replied in a small, reproachful voice.

'Have you studied the form?'

'I certainly have,' she said in the same small voice. 'Did you bring the flask?'

I patted my pocket.

'Right then, Harold,' she said, with a curt nod of her head.

It was another attempt at normal life. Another attempt at getting involved. A fishing trip with my father; an afternoon at the races with my aged promiscuous aunt.

Her version of normal had always made sense to me. Her subversive streak was a great attraction. When I was a child and was dumped on her during my summer holidays she didn't complain. I innocently assumed that she didn't complain because she was a Quaker. I remember she took me into a Catholic church one hot summer's day and showed me a confession box. 'Now,' she said, opening the door, 'this is where Mr Punch lives.'

She had got me an hour's work in the local cinema. I was given a stick of chalk. The job was to test the seats for squeaks. I sat in each in turn, pressed my body into the backrest and vigorously rocked back and forth. I was to mark the ones that squeaked with my stick of chalk. I got five pounds for the job. Five pounds was an extraordinarily generous sum, but then the cinema owner was one of Aunt Kate's many doubtful lovers. I knew this because she had told me so.

It was my first illicit money, as I thought. My first bob-a-job. I put an X on the backs of squeaking seats in a picture house belonging to one of my Aunt Kate's fancy men.

Horse racing doesn't much excite me, but I was content to be there. It was television out of its box. There was a lesson here, as with the fishing. I just couldn't quite grasp what I was to learn. However, I did recognise that, if you didn't get involved, there was a comfortable monotony to it, and there was always the outside chance that others' excitement would be momentarily infectious.

We were too late to bet on the first race. We paid the extra few pounds to get into the reserved enclosure. Before the second race we watched the horses parade. Kate read aloud from her race card, convinced that I had failed to grasp the significance of the one-line notes under each listing. Because of the recent rain the going was displayed as 'Soft'.

'Watch out for the size of their hooves,' she said, out of the side of her mouth. 'The larger the hooves the better they fare on the soft ground.'

'Right,' I said. 'Large hooves.'

She pointed to one owner listed on her card.

'Stay clear of his stable,' she said. 'Terrible showing all round. It must have a bug.'

I acknowledged the name.

We returned to the enclosure to watch the horses parade before each of the remaining races. Throughout the afternoon we moved from the enclosure, to the bookies, to the terrace. Kate frequently thought people were addressing their remarks to her. That had her smiling politely in all directions as a cover for not having quite caught what it was they had said.

She placed her bets down at the track instead of at the window. She liked the business of choosing her moment and making her wager quickly. She liked the clothes the bookies and their accountants wore, and she liked to parade herself in front of them. She wanted me out of earshot because she was betting larger sums than she would admit to.

I was down by the track when the commentator's even voice began to balloon out of the public address system for the fifth race. The horses started at the far end of the straight. I turned to take in the crowd on the terrace. There was a steady stream of people mounting and descending the steps. In the body of the standing figures almost all faces were turned to the far end of the track. Many were using binoculars. There were a few scribbling notes. A few distracted by children. There was just one looking at me.

He was a sandy-haired man in his forties. He was standing halfway up the terrace. He had a pair of binoculars sitting on his chest.

Was I sure he was looking at me? Was he aware that

I was scrutinising him? I moved forwards several paces then stopped.

'Harold, you're a fool for not listening to me. Look – she's way out in front.'

I glanced back to Kate for just a moment, but when I looked again to the terrace my man had vanished and there was no gap in the rank. I looked again to Kate. What was she saying? I had fire in my ears.

'Oh Christ,' she exclaimed. 'Look at this other one . . .'

I went through the motions of betting on each race and broke even overall. Kate won more than she lost. She would not say how much she had accumulated.

Such was my sense of being closely observed, I felt that had I the opportunity to ask my sandy-haired man he would have whispered in my ear an accurate total for Kate's winnings.

In any case, he must have got what he had come for.

Before leaving the race track I went to a public telephone intending to ring Alfie. I had had time to think, but I still wasn't sure what I was going to say. Something along the lines of – You're not right for that job. You're a sick man. You're a bastard for deceiving me, but you're my friend. Do I have to recite the villain's motto?

It must have been friendship that motivated the call, because Toby Harquin's fate wasn't a consideration.

I rang Alfie's mobile telephone. He had it switched off. I rang the number for the telephone in the hall above the Earls Court basement. Nobody answered it.

*　　*　　*

I took Kate home. She pressed thirty pounds into my hand. She insisted on sharing her winnings – it would bring us both good luck, she told me. What was it that made people want to give me tax-free earnings and pocket money?

She offered me the flask we had filled but had not touched.

'You should have that tonight,' I said. 'To celebrate.'

'All right,' she said. 'I will.'

She got out of the car but then leant back in.

'I just thought if I gave it to you you might return it.'

'I had a lovely day, Kate. I'll see you again soon. I will.'

'Remember, darling, I know a thing or two.'

She closed the door, then shouted through the window, '*And* I can get you another wife.'

'Yes-yes,' I heard Uberto's muffled voice say, 'he is here. He is upstairs.'

Whoever it was, they had pressed the wrong doorbell, inadvertently or otherwise.

My door was locked – I inserted my pocket wedges for added resistance. As I heard the footfalls on the staircase I moved quickly to the bay windows. I keep a small rectangular mirror to hand in the flat. Crouching down, I held it discreetly at an angle just above the bottom of each window frame. It was a procedure I had rehearsed. It enabled me to scan both ends of the street without being seen. I was looking for chaps in a stationary car or van. Two men watching – like Alfie and me.

I could see none.

There was a rap on the door.

'Hey, Harry,' Uberto said, trying to sound considerate and efficient, 'somebody here to see you.'

I was about to use my escape route – out through the bathroom window to the drainpipe that led down to the yard and the lane or up on to the roof. The roof was a last resort. There was a two-brick high parapet with a granite capstone and a hole for the gutter to drain into the downpipe. This made the journey possible, but the parapet's bricks were crumbling. I had a vision of bricks crumbling under my elbows. Down, I had decided, when I heard a woman's voice calling my name through the door. I recognised it instantly.

'Harry, it's me – Ruth.'

I swiftly removed the wedges, unlocked the door and threw it open. I gave her as warm a greeting as I could bluster. It must have sounded fitting because Uberto was evidently very happy to witness the reunion.

I was already jumpy. Ruth's visit took me completely by surprise. It was Sunday night. The theatre was closed. I hadn't got further than that.

She stood in the middle of the room and looked about her, her beautiful long bones radiant under her pale skin. I couldn't have her examining this shabby interior, however uncritical her gaze. I couldn't have her thinking this place was anything more than a temporary base.

She had come without any luggage. To anyone else she might have appeared to be lost.

'Comfortable,' she said.

'Oh yes,' I replied, leading her over to an armchair. 'But I've a lot in storage . . .'

Oh yes – a container full of suburban furniture and a flock of life-sized porcelain swans.

'. . . I'll be out of here soon. There's a dentist moving in . . .'

'Harry, I'm so worried about Alfie,' she said. 'I tried calling you but there was no answer.'

She had sat down but now she was on her feet again and her eyes were filling with tears. 'He came to the house in a terrible state. All cut and bruised.'

I put a comforting hand on her shoulder. I had a picture of Alfie standing in his suburban doorway, just as I had stood. I saw him looking at his wife from under swollen eyelids. He was bent over his own shadow. His feet were stuck to the ground, but there was a subtle, unbroken movement in his battered torso. I saw his eyes drop from Ruth's face to monitor his swaying. He was testing to see if his shadow left a stain on the far side of the threshold.

I saw Ruth reaching out to him.

'What's happening?' she said to me. 'You can tell me. He would say nothing.'

I gave her a drink, which I poured from the flask. It was the only spirits I had in the flat. I let her drink in silence. It was early evening. There were still several hours of light.

'Come on,' I said, when she had finished. 'We'll talk in the car.'

Now that Ruth was sitting beside me again in a car I had the curious sense that anything I said would be a repetition.

I got out of a tight parking space with skill I didn't know I possessed. I worked the steering wheel like a fork-lift operator. I wasn't sure where I would take her. I wanted her out of the flat. Perhaps we would just drive and talk.

I drove out of the city towards the mountains. For a time a kestrel scouted ahead of us, keeping a constant distance. It used the updraught of warm, polluted air from the dual carriageway to glide. It abandoned us when we struck off the main route and began to climb. This was a familiar road, but a road that was never the same distance twice. I recognised now that we were on our way to where the fires had raged.

'What has he told you?' I asked.

'Nothing. I've told you – nothing.'

'All right . . .'

'It's something to do with the money he's taken, isn't it? They're never going to leave him alone, are they? Nobody will do a damn thing to protect him. They're going to kill him.'

'Nobody is out to kill anybody, Ruth . . .'

'You can help him. Whatever he's said or done to send you away, please forgive him . . .'

'We've been working on a job.' I quickly corrected myself, 'A case – surveillance . . . and that's finished with.'

'Those bastards on the force won't help him. He respects you. Help him, Harry. He's always counted you as his friend. He's helped you, hasn't he? Whatever he's done wrong, he doesn't deserve this.'

'I'll do what I can.'

'You know people. You can make things stop. These gangsters must be afraid of what you can do.'

There was no denying that I wanted her with me. I had brooded on the prospect. I had a picture of her swimming in a lake. In this picture her slender limbs sent out a circle of ripples that broadcast her ease with sex. The cold seemed not to bother her. I could not have imagined such a sight from looking at her china swan in her porthole window. Her swimming was intended to drive me to distraction, and she swam until she was exhausted. It was a picture I repeatedly summoned, but it always ended with me waking in the middle of the night shuddering with the cold. The blood in her muscles and in her veins could no longer keep me warm, and so I looked for the brilliant white bones of her cellist's fingers to light up the dark.

Now, she was telling me that her husband's enemies must be afraid of what I could do.

I suppose I was surprised that she was more loyal than I, in spite of our brief assignation.

We got out of the car and climbed on to an outcrop on the side of a mountain. There were runs of exposed roots that formed steps. We gazed at the blackened landscape that was already beginning to sprout wisps of green. Ruth continued with her fretful account of Alfie's decline. She continued to flatter me and to assert our friendship. Her words rotated as they left her lips, suggesting that their true meaning was concealed, but, nonetheless, available to me. The affair she imagined for us, the affair I secretly wanted to make a reality, was to be suspended.

I said that I would return to London with her. She kissed me deeply. It was some kind of a promise.

On our way back to the city I caught myself filling the silence with a tuneless humming. I was humming to cover my wild speculation as to what the next forty-eight hours would bring.

'Go on,' she said, smiling.

'No,' I said, 'you sing.'

She told me that she could not sing, but I knew already that this was untrue, for she had a melodious laugh.

She did sing. In a distant, melodious voice sent to haunt me. 'The Parting Glass' – it was a traditional song I had not heard before. The singing, too, was part of the promise.

We had an Indian take-away dinner, watching a party in the windows of the house next to the vacant site. While I was packing a few things the telephone rang. We both froze for the first two rings.

'Harry, it's me.'

'I know it's you.'

'I'm all right.'

'So you tell me. But have you got sense yet?'

There was a hesitation at the other end of the line. My heart contracted into a bloodless knot. Had he already done it? Had he killed Toby Harquin?

'I don't like this,' he said. 'I'm on my own.'

'I thought you were coming to visit me. Spoil another fishing trip.'

'Slack period for you, eh? They don't have you pulling stunts?'

'No. No stunts.'

Ruth was watching me. Measuring every word.

Alfie continued. It was the same cocky individual who had greeted me on the lake shore. The same easy patter. The same marzipan pig with a few lumps out of him. I could tell he was trying not to drink, but he was getting nostalgic for our 'carefree' drinking spree that had ended with his cardiac arrest, and that was very disturbing.

I knew he wasn't interested in any kind of reform. I had learnt that in the hospital. His dangerous big-man behaviour was fuelled by self-pity. His priorities had become confused and I could see no spark that might lead him clear of that confusion. He was faring badly as a dry drunk. I wanted to help him but was confused myself. I was returning Ruth's look now, making a vague and empty gesture with my hand to indicate that all would be well.

'Where are you now?'

'I'm at home.'

'Why don't you answer that damn phone?'

'Not in the flat, Harry. *Home*. You remember. Where I live with my wife.'

I missed a beat. It didn't matter because Ruth could hear what was being said. She could hear his small, metallic voice.

'Will you switch on that mobile phone. Christ almighty – what's the point of having it if you don't switch it on.'

'Harry . . . she's having an affair.'

'Oh, come on . . .'

'I've really fucked everything up, haven't I?'

'You're not living with her. Stop feeling sorry for yourself.'

The words stung my throat. I had to turn my back on Ruth. I couldn't bear to see the light drain from her face.

'You're not thinking straight, Alfie . . .'

'No, Harry, you're wrong. It's all perfectly clear now. I'm calling to let you in on the picture . . . to give you the news . . .'

'What news?'

'Our missing woman has turned up on her own doorstep. She's come home to her loving husband, Toby. And you want to know where's she's been, don't you?'

'Do I?'

'The past few days Daddy's been hiding her.'

'What?'

'Sydney has been protecting her. Nobody knows where she's been before that. She won't speak about it.'

'The woman has been missing a full month . . .'

'Happens all the time. Damaged people disappearing . . .'

I turned a finger in the air impatiently to get him straight to the facts.

'Three nights ago she turns up on her father's doorstep.'

'Three nights ago . . . ?'

'Look – Toby Harquin has been torturing her, so one night she runs away. She goes to her friend with the flat in Soho. She stays just one night then she disappears. She's not well, Harry. She's been beaten around the house by that thug of a husband because he's a thug and maybe because she's having some kind of breakdown . . .'

'Are you telling me Holland has kept her return a secret from the police?'

'I saw him nursing her. He called me to his house. He wanted me to see what had been done to his baby – his words . . . He's heartbroken, and he's very, very angry.'

'What – he had her locked in a room?'

'He was nursing her . . .'

'Christ . . .'

'He's had her there for three nights because he just couldn't let go of her . . . but she goes anyway. She runs back to her husband. She finds out about Claire and the back seat of Toby's car. She can't bear it, so she runs home to make a fresh start.'

'Holland's told the police now?'

'They know she went back to the Chelsea house. They know she has a mental problem. You'll see it in the papers tomorrow – *Missing Woman Returns*. There won't be details.'

'You're finished, then? Finished with Holland?'

'All I have to bother about is making a living.'

'I'm coming back.'

'It'll be nice to see you again. We can go on the town. Sydney has paid me the money we're due. I have something for you in an envelope. What do you think I could do that would help me put things right with Ruth? Maybe you could put in a word with your lot up the river – get me a job. You'd make a lousy copper, Harry, but I'd be good at doing what you do.'

His humour was too bitter to raise even the faintest smile.

'Switch on the mobile phone, Alfie.'

CHAPTER 16

I lifted an early edition of *The Times* from a business class seat. It was as Alfie had predicted – a brief article reporting Vanessa Harquin's mysterious disappearance and the bare fact that she had returned home.

During the flight I got Ruth to tell me what she knew about Alfie's relationship with Sydney Holland. It transpired that she knew next to nothing. He had done some security work for him, she told me. He had vetted bodyguards for some of his clients. He had checked to see if they had police records.

Perhaps that was all there was to it, but I had my doubts.

'How did things get like this, Harry?'

I shrugged.

'He's been a bloody fool,' she continued. 'Always trying to please me. It drives me crazy. It's double the pressure when I'm not working.'

'A little extra. That's his favourite number. You know that.'

'He wants to move house again. "Something nicer," he says. "Somewhere better . . ."'

'Well, you know I'll be moving . . .' The remark came out without my thinking. It was meant to be an illustration of man's desire to improve conditions for himself generally, not a special plea.

'We can't have children, Harry, but he wants a bigger house.'

I saw her eyes widen to avoid shedding tears. I put my hand on hers, but she slipped hers away.

'All this attention focused on me . . .' she said.

It was a strange complaint, but I knew exactly what she meant.

'We'll get him straight, Ruth,' I said.

She nodded. I could tell she wanted to say that her relationship with Alfie was still wholly intact, but she held back. I was taken by her resilience; her dogged optimism. I glanced at her lap, then I drew up my wrist so that I would have to look at my watch.

I bought the rest of the papers at Heathrow. They all carried similar reports on Holland's daughter's return. I rang Alfie's mobile number before we left for the city. He had his phone switched off.

We went straight to the house with the swan. Ruth called out his name as she pushed open the hall door, but Alfie wasn't there and he hadn't left a note.

I put my things in the spare bedroom. I rang the mobile again. Still switched off. I dialled the number for the phone in the hall above the Earls Court flat. Nobody answered. I got Ruth to ring one of Alfie's colleagues at the station. Nobody there had seen or talked to him since the seven-a-side match.

I drove to Earls Court in Ruth's car. The flat smelt of damp, and sour milk. There was nothing in the place to indicate that Alfie had been there that morning, but, given his behaviour, a normal pattern didn't apply. In any case, it hadn't applied when we were both living in the kip.

The tap was drizzling in the poky bathroom under the hall steps. A small slug was working its way down the white wall. It seemed to be in a hurry.

I went to the coin-operated phone in the hall upstairs and rang Alfie's mobile number again.

Off.

I took a quick walk around the neighbourhood. His car wasn't parked anywhere in the vicinity.

I berated Alfie for being so selfish as I drove by the river towards Chelsea. He was wasting my time, I decided. He had climbed back into the bottle somewhere and was justifying himself to the world with his scribblings in his greasy notebook.

I was sure about his condition. I was not sure about the rest. I hoped he was railing at the world in his notebook, not hunched in a corner talking to his hammerless gun.

I drove past the Harquin house. All the curtains at the front of the house were drawn. There were a lot of people sitting in cars, none of them Alfie. All of them with cameras, pocket recorders and mobile phones.

Ruth rang everyone she thought he might stay with. No one she contacted had seen him recently.

Eventually, we went to our beds. I lay down in the spare room and waited for the telephone to ring. At some point I fell asleep, but I woke up shivering in the small hours. Ruth slept fitfully, if at all. I could hear her tossing and turning. I called her name just once, but she didn't answer. The phone didn't ring.

Ms Twitter was deploying her words with great precision. She was speaking in complete sentences, each word distinct, but with them all concertinaed into machine-gun fire, as though she were delivering an exercise for typists.

She had been fending off the press all day and was still doing a good job, but now she was punch-drunk. She was telling me the same story she had been telling everybody else, nothing more than the bare facts that had already appeared in the papers. Mr Holland's daughter had returned to the family bosom and was now being cared for. Mr Holland and his former wife were delighted and hugely relieved. The police were thanked for their tremendous effort. A full statement would be issued in time.

I reminded her that I had been working for Mr Holland, but this made no impression. She kept up with the publicity line. I could have taken off my ears and put them in my pocket and she wouldn't have noticed.

'Look,' I said, 'I know what's happened. I need to see Mr Holland immediately. Tell him it's about our mutual friend Alfie.'

Holland agreed to see me. It would be only for a short time. He was on his way to visit his daughter.

I didn't want to talk to him in his office. I insisted he come out on to the street. Reluctantly, he agreed.

He lumbered down the staircase in front of me. His slowness was an assertion of his desire to manage the event.

We walked a few yards in the street. He stopped to buy a paper at a news-stand. It was inconceivable that a copy of the same paper had not already been delivered to his office. When we moved on he made ground half a step ahead of me. He was now leading the way, just as he had done on the stairs.

He glanced at the headlines. He quietly made a show of scanning through the contents of the newspaper. He pointed to one article which reported the racist remarks of a back-bencher.

'You see this one,' he said. 'His wife thought it would be a good idea if I worked with her husband on his image problem, but I declined. When it comes to officials I'm happier dealing with the corrupt ones. I try to avoid the fascists.'

It was an interesting distinction. It seemed to preclude the possibility of a corrupt fascist.

'Civil servant or politician,' he added. 'You would agree . . . ?'

This, of course, was an indirect reference to Alfie.

'Yes,' I said, 'when it comes to that, I'm for the crook every time.'

I didn't feel the same need to be vague.

'I don't know what favours Alfie has done for you in the past,' I said. 'Nor do I particularly give a damn, but I know he's out there now killing himself for you.'

He took his time responding. He led me to a bench under a grubby tree on a traffic island. He had a good instinct for the clandestine talk. I couldn't have picked a better spot in the district myself. He took up a position at one end of the bench. This was his bench, not mine. There was no pigeon shit where he sat. This was Sydney

Holland demonstrating that the pigeons knew not to shit on any part of his domain.

'You have me confused with a football manager,' he said.

'Don't fuck with me, Sydney. You want him to kill that thug you have for a son-in-law.'

'I'm shocked that you would say such a thing.' For all his staging of our exchange, he was already growing agitated. I could understand that. He was in his own, private hell and he was wearing his special voice, by turns sharp, then dangerously vague.

'And he told you I would do it.'

'You have such a talent? How very interesting.'

Holland had been relying on Alfie, but then Alfie had been relying on me.

'I'm here to tell you it's not going to happen.'

I was back outside the pub with Alfie. I was having to tell somebody who was threatening my damaged friend that Alfie was stupid, but Alfie was with me.

We both knew that making overt threats was, as a rule, unwise. If for no other reason than that to issue threats was to give warning.

'You've got your troubles. Alfie's got his troubles. He's a sick man.'

'I know about the poisoning.'

'And now he has heart problems.'

'I know about his heart attack.'

'He's not thinking straight and that's bad news for you, Sydney, any way you look at it.'

'Alfie has finished his work for me. My daughter is – safe. You've both done a thorough job. I'm grateful.

Had Vanessa not returned you would have found her, I know.'

'When did you last talk to him?'

'Last week,' he replied, his voice suddenly becoming vague. He was signalling that this was an end to it, as far as he was concerned.

He returned to his newspaper, but now with the slow, gawky fish eyes he cultivated. It was an infuriating encounter. He was behaving as though his discretion was being tested. He bristled, but he admired thoroughness. He would never have tolerated his resolve being questioned.

'If he contacts you again, you reel him in and you call me at this number.' I gave him Alfie's home telephone number.

'If he contacts me, I'll tell him you would like to talk to him.'

'You do that.'

There was an awkward silence. Awkward for me, that is.

'Thank you,' he said.

He behaved like any one of a dozen men shopping alone I had passed on my way to the Men's Department.

'Very pleased to see you again, sir,' he said, shaking my hand.

I had not met this one before, but he came recommended. The pretence that we had met before was typical of encounters with his sort. They feel the need for some concrete demonstration of their discretion.

'Now, look,' he said, momentarily resting his fist

under his chin, 'you don't mind . . . I need to buy a new coat.'

'No. I don't mind.'

'Very good. Now, let me see – coats would be – this way, I think. Yes.'

I went with him to the coat rails.

'I shan't be long,' he said. 'I know what I like.'

'Take your time.'

'Oh but I can't do that, you see. My wife – she isn't well and I've the shopping to do.'

'Here,' I said, 'let me help you. What size? You like this colour . . . ?'

I hadn't dealt with this one before but I knew his type would want to take the coat off its hanger himself, so I just pointed.

He was a fussy man. Slightly effeminate but, so far as I could judge, steely underneath. He wasn't at all like Freddie. I had gone to Freddie first but he had retired to his apple orchard in Kent. He was having nothing more to do with it. If I had thought about it I would have taken this as a bad omen. So I didn't think about it.

Freddie had given me the man's mobile number as a special favour.

'Shan't be long.'

He had said that twice now.

'That looks good.'

'No.'

He got me to help him on with a coat. Freddie would never have embarrassed me like that.

'There now,' he said, 'that's more like it.' Without breaking the rhythm of his voice, he added – 'What is it you want?'

I told him what I wanted.

'I see,' he said, turning from one side to the other, viewing himself in the new coat in a tall mirror.

A shop assistant approached. Our man held up his hand.

'No need,' he said theatrically, 'you'll be called.'

The assistant moved away with lips compressed.

'You have a fixed mind on the matter?' he asked me.

'No. I'll look at anything similar.'

'Similar . . . yes . . .'

I knew what he was getting at. He wanted to know if I was going to war.

'Just the one piece,' I said. 'With one clip.'

'Very good. Now. I'm going to buy this coat. If you could just bear with me . . .'

When I had told him that I wanted a Beretta he had knit his brow and shaken his head. Was he trying to impress me? Was he telling me he had had a run on Berettas?

In his car he told me he could get me a Beretta, but it would take forty-eight hours. He was wearing his new coat. He had his old coat in the department store bag. According to my watch it was too warm to wear any kind of a coat.

He showed me a Smith & Wesson Magnum.

I shook my head slowly.

'I know you said you wanted an automatic, but please, wouldn't you like to . . . weigh this?'

I told him I didn't want anything that required the boot of a car for a holster.

He offered me a Walther. It had the characteristics

I was looking for, but I didn't like the double action required for the first shot. He watched me handle it.

'Ah yes,' he said with a generous measure of satisfaction, 'you like that . . .'

Freddie, I thought, this monkey makes me nervous and you should have known better than to recommend him.

'*You* like the Walther?' I asked, with a strong note of scepticism.

'I don't like any of them,' he replied blandly.

I scoffed.

He was offended.

I was in a hurry. I bought the Walther and wished his wife well.

The paths through the unlikely array of vegetation were rutted from the feet of generations of gardeners, and their wheelbarrows. I could understand how that would appeal to a man like Alfie, who often trod unsafe ground.

I recognised carrot, spinach, cabbage and potato drills. There were other shoots that seemed to me as likely to be found growing out of the cracks in a chimney stack. I could walk here with Alfie and like it, I thought, in spite of my ignorance.

I imagined him crossing paths with retired bankers. People with friends who could supply him with manure. Young men with dogs on ropes, who pestered the older diggers for tips while the dogs pissed on their brassicas.

Over by the electricity pylon, Ruth had said. The pylon was anchored on a gentle rise. Beneath the tower there was a little shanty town of rickety sheds and makeshift greenhouses. I made my way towards the pylon. In the distance I could see a woman on her knees weeding what looked like a neglected cemetery plot. Above her there was a stand of sunflowers I was sure were made of plastic and paper. I passed aubergines, chillies and tomatoes under glass that had a thin green scum on the inside of the panes.

It was early evening. There were sparrows twitching violently and beating their wings in short, manic bursts on the dry soil around the edges of the path. Their noise unnerved me. I came upon an abandoned thermos. There was a bee buzzing in it. I tapped it with my foot. The bee flew out and away. As I followed its progress I caught sight of the washed-out crimson door hanging crooked in its frame. The entrance to Alfie's bolt-hole. Only the upper hinge was firmly secured. There was a small window set beside the door. The shed was wedged between a dense, thorny hedge and an old apple tree, the branches of which brushed Alfie's corrugated iron roof.

I stood for a moment looking at the place. I was startled by an elderly Bangladeshi man with a brilliant white beard who emerged from a side path. He greeted me with a curt but polite 'Hello', which I instantly returned. He moved past me without breaking his stride. The tops of root vegetables protruded from his bulging anorak pockets. He was carrying two heads of cabbage.

Yes, I thought, Alfie would be comfortable among this diversity of monkish people.

Without good reason, I was convinced that I would

find him here waiting for me. He would be sitting in an old easy chair, the bottom of which had burst. He would have his feet up on a kitchen chair that had lost its back. He would put down his cup of tea and bark some insult at me and pretend to be unhappy with my disturbing his convalescence.

I looked through the window. I could see an old hammock slung from corner to corner and a vacant chair. Unless he was hunched in the near corner, there was nowhere else he could position himself without my seeing him.

It was easy to gain entry, but this was an intrusion. It wasn't like breaking and entering Toby Harquin's Chelsea house.

He wasn't there, but I whispered Alfie's name. I turned about slowly. There were gardening tools, a pile of paperback novels and instruction manuals, and old newspapers. Last year's calendar hung on the wall. Some tinned food on a shelf. A supermarket carrier bag containing empty tins and food packaging. There was a Primus stove with a small pot. There was no kitchen chair without a back, but there was a mug without a handle. He had been drinking tea out of that. There was tea in the bottom of it. I dipped my finger in the dregs. The liquid was slightly warmer than room temperature. He had been there all right, and not long before.

I found the walkie-talkies and the other items he had taken from the railway locker wrapped in a piece of sacking. Only the gun was missing.

I rang Ruth to tell her I would be continuing my search and not to expect me back that night. I had no choice but to resume my surveillance of Toby Harquin in anticipation of Alfie showing up with a gun in his hand. Ruth told me that Alfie had just rung her on his mobile telephone. He didn't want her worrying about him. He had told her that he loved her and that he had, at last, got sense. He wouldn't tell her where he was. He would only say that he would be coming home.

I rang the mobile number again.

Alfie answered.

'Harrry . . .'

'Alfie, where are you?'

'Are you looking out for me again? You're a pal.'

'Where are you?'

'I'm watching Toby. I can see him right now. He's eating his dinner.'

He was drinking again. That had been confirmed by his first words.

'Where?'

'I'm across the street. He's taken his daughter out. He'll want to spoil her, don't you think? Just to take her mind off her poor mother. The mother's in hospital. Did I tell you?'

'I know. And you're finished with all of that.'

'You know the beating I got . . .'

'Yes.'

'Not the poisoning, not the shafting by my fellow officers, the beating . . .'

'Yes, I know. The beating you got . . .'

'I think some of that was meant for you.'

'Really . . .'

'It feels like it. Don't get me wrong – I'm all right . . .'

'So you keep telling me.'

'But I've taken enough. You agree?'

'Yes. You've had enough.'

'I've just talked to Ruth . . .'

'Go home, Alfie.'

'She's a remarkable woman . . .'

'I know. Go home.'

'She's working that cello even as we speak . . .'

'Where are you?'

'I'm helping a friend, Harry.'

'Holland's daughter is sick and now she's being looked after. That changes everything.'

'Harry, you're not thinking. Toby – the one who made her sick – his work is never done.'

'I'll come with you – just tell me where you are.'

'Do you know, I think I've had dinner with Sydney in that place . . . yes . . .'

'Alfie . . . please . . .'

There was a pause, then he muttered – 'I thought I'd switched this thing off . . .'

The connection went dead.

I observed Toby return to his house with his daughter. I watched for Alfie, but he did not present himself. I rang Ruth just after midnight. Alfie had not gone home. In the small hours I returned to the allotments, thinking I would find him there, but his shed was vacant.

The following morning Toby drove his daughter back to her boarding school.

As the streets lights came on that evening, once again I found myself sitting in a car at the end of the street in

Chelsea, getting a stiff neck trying to keep a clear line of vision.

At three o'clock in the morning I woke with a shudder. A short time later I saw Toby's thugs emerge from the house. The two of them moved quickly in my direction. They were searching the street for something. I got out of the car smartly, turned on my heels and moved away from them before they got a close look at me. I turned the nearest corner and hid in the first basement stairwell that had an open gate. I watched them pass the mouth of the street. It was clear by the way they were scouring the neighbourhood that they were looking for a car. When they had passed from view I surfaced to followed them.

Several streets away they found what they were looking for, and my heart seized momentarily. It was Alfie's car. I felt nauseous when I saw one of them insert the key in the door.

I think I let out a strangled utterance that might have been Alfie's name, and that was how the new thinking came to resemble the old, and became indistinguishable.

I began walking back towards Harquin's house. Twice, I stopped by the railings. Could I have it wrong? Perhaps they had Alfie tied to a chair. He had blundered in there with his gun and they had overpowered him. If that was what I believed, why was I choking with rage and an instant grief? I had been asleep for about two and a half hours. That was more than enough time to put a body down some stinking culvert. They could have waltzed him out the front door and sat him up in the back seat of their car.

Hank Williams was singing to himself in the living room. As I advanced through the hall I could hear Harquin on the telephone down in the kitchen. I started with the rooms upstairs and worked my way down. It was all as it had been before. I could barely resist an urge to call out for my friend. If they had him tied to a chair it would be in the basement, I assured myself.

When I returned to the staircase leading to the kitchen Harquin was still talking on the telephone. I waited on the landing.

Alfie, Alfie, Alfie.

When the man had ceased talking and had put down the receiver, I descended the stairs.

He was startled, but had the presence of mind to challenge me with nothing more than a posture. He didn't need to take in details. He remembered my face. There was no trace of Alfie. No smell of him. No sign of a struggle. Everything was in its place and there was a smell of pine-scented cleaning fluid.

'Alfie,' I said.

'Alfie?' he replied with a big question mark.

'Yes. Alfie.' That was everything I had to say.

He had nothing to say to me. He gave me an all-embracing shrug, so I took out the Walther and shot him twice.

I had done what had been expected of me, but too late to save Alfie. Had I thought about it I would have been sickened by the knowledge that this was to be my redemption.

So I didn't think about it. Instead, I went on talking to my crooked friend.

CHAPTER 17

Ruth got a call from Alfie's mother. She wasn't coping well with her son's disappearance. Nor was her decrepit husband. He was outside, attempting to start their car. The car had been rotting in the garage since he had, effectively, been banned from driving several years before.

'He's out there now,' she wailed, 'and he won't listen to me. He thinks he can go looking for Alfie in that bloody car. I've told Alfie he should get rid of it.'

The battery was flat, of course. The old man hadn't been able to get it started. He was in with the next-door neighbour looking to get a jump-start.

The old woman was in a dreadful panic. Ruth and I went to the house immediately. By the time we arrived Alfie's father was back in his garage. He was, he thought, going to push the vehicle – a heavy Vauxhall saloon – out into the street to a position that would allow the battery of the neighbour's car to be connected to his with the jump-leads.

'Come and help me,' he called out when he saw us.

We got him inside. Ruth talked calmly to both of them while she made them tea. She tried to reassure them when, really, she was as distressed as they were.

The old man had let the handbrake off, and had managed to get the rear wheels of the Vauxhall out beyond the garage door only because there was a slight rake to the drive. He had an old set of jump-leads with insulation that was falling away on the front passenger seat.

While they were inside I pushed the car back into the garage with the help of the teenager from next door. He had been the only one in when Alfie's father had knocked on the door. He had taken his mother's car out of their garage for the jump-start.

I thanked him and told him that the old man was anxious to make a journey that just wasn't feasible.

'I was wondering,' the young man said nervously. 'He told me he needed the car for Alfie. I told him he'd better wait for Alfie to arrive, but he insisted he wanted the battery charged up . . .'

When he had gone I shut the garage door and disabled the car. I ensured that no amount of jump-starting would see the engine kick into life.

Initially, my father fretted. My coming to visit again so soon was a mistake, perhaps. But he seemed to overcome his anxiety when I told him I would not be staying. I was numbed. Numbness helped to bear the burden of being the only one who could mourn for Alfie. For the others there was only the cruel suspension and the pain that had to be challenged each day, and that challenge would be the measure of hope.

'You can stay as long as you want,' Cecil said.

'I know that.'

I stood in the kitchen eating cereal from a bowl that I held under my chin. I watched the old man eat a boiled egg mashed in a cup with breadcrumbs, butter and pepper. He managed to do this without inviting any pity. In fact, there was a sorry-there-aren't-any-more-eggs smugness to his eating.

'There's been burglaries,' he said. 'Three houses on this side of the street in a fortnight . . .'

None of his neighbours had exchanged intelligence on the matter, he informed me. He had learnt about the break-ins at the shop where he bought his newspaper.

Perhaps this was what had him upset.

'Came in through the roof each time,' he said. 'The roof is the most vulnerable in these houses. In most houses,' he added. 'Of course, you'd know that.' There was no trace of irony in his remark, though I might have expected it.

'In most houses,' I mumbled.

'I was thinking of getting some kind of alarm.'

He looked down at the ancient dog under the kitchen table, then his eyes slowly came up to meet mine.

What – did he want me to take the animal to the vet to get it put down? It hadn't barked when I rang the bell. It had scarcely stirred when I entered the house. It was useless as a watchdog. Christ. I hoped he didn't want that.

No. The awkward silence was for another reason. He told me he had somebody coming to stay.

Kate?

No. A friend.

What kind of friend? An expatriate? A destitute crony? Who?

A woman.

What did he mean – stay?

She was moving in. He didn't want the house alarm for himself.

'Moving in.' They were his words. I was shocked.

'Are you sure?' I blurted out.

He repeated my question to indicate its absurdity.

I had to smile. Then, I had to laugh. Then, I shook his hand. He was hugely relieved.

He didn't describe her. He didn't tell me that I would like her. Instead, he patted me on the shoulder. He threw our dishes in the sink. Then he humped his coat on to his back and shuffled and rotated in the hall.

'Come on,' he said. 'We'll go for a drink.'

I joined him at the top of the hall and for a moment we were both framed in the mirror.

'You'd like that?' He asked my reflection. He paid no attention to his own.

'I'd like that,' I said.

He smelt sweeter than he had for a long time. Perhaps that was why the dog had generally given up. Cecil had resumed his twice-weekly trips to the Turkish baths where he and his companions soaped each other down, and dozed wrapped in towels when they had finished with the hot air and the washing and the kneading. The woman moving in had to be a reality. I could not assume that he would tell me about her. He was getting more contrary. I would be invited to inspect the newly installed alarm. That was how he would introduce her.

We walked at our ease.

'All cities have their night flush,' he said, looking up into the sky. 'Something that pervades the dark.'

By day he was seeing shapes in the clouds. Now, he

was seeing an aurora laid on especially for him in the night sky.

'Oh yes . . . ?' I said, glancing up, '. . . and London?'

'A dirty magenta.'

'Like when you close your eyes . . .' I suggested without thinking, '. . . the black isn't really black . . .'

'It's got nothing to do with closing your eyes. Nothing to do with the blackness of sleep. When you wake from sleep it's never where you left off. It isn't like that. This is constant, but it only registers at night.'

I had never heard him talk like this before.

He asked about Kate. I told him about our day at the races.

'You can tell her about Rita,' he volunteered. This was the first time he'd mentioned his new companion's name.

'I will.'

'I've talked to Kate,' he confessed.

'Really?' I feigned surprise.

'She tells me you're seeing somebody.'

I shrugged.

'Good. I'm glad to hear it.'

He wanted to ask questions but held back. It made things easier – I couldn't think what I might say.

'I'll meet her when I visit again.'

'Yes. I hope so.'

'You haven't told me about the house you live in.'

'Well . . . I'll be moving . . .'

'They want you back here?'

'Well no . . . not yet.'

'Not yet . . . I see.'

'You'll have to come and visit me again – both of you will have to come,' I quickly added. 'When I have the new place.'

'Yes. That would be the thing, wouldn't it.'

There was a brief silence, then he looked at me just as he had looked at the dog under the table.

'You should give up that game,' he said earnestly. 'Do something else. It doesn't matter what kind of a job.'

'You're right,' I said, answering quickly.

I began to lead, half a pace ahead.

My sincere hope was that Ruth would contact me some day soon. I resolved that I would not wait indefinitely. *I* would call *her* and invite myself back into her life.

Her waiting for Alfie to come home was the hardest thing to bear. I *would* ring her. I had a strong urge to turn around instantly and go back for her, but I knew that she would not have come with me, nor could I have stayed. I would have to be patient. I would speak to her regularly on the telephone to ask if there was any news, and one day she would call me and the conversation would be different, and I would cease talking to Alfie while I drove my car.

The woman upstairs had gone. Uberto had also left, taking his mysterious grip bag with him. As it turned out, the dentist was bona fide, but he only wanted Uberto's ground-floor flat for his practice. The landlord wanted rid of us all so that he could raise the rent. I had moved my belongings out, though I had not yet found a new flat. I was storing my things at Kate's house.

I went back to the flat to take the beehive door handle.

I met a young woman waiting on the doorstep with a child. She mistook me for the landlord.

'Not me,' I told her. 'I'm just moving out. You're not looking at the first-floor flat, are you?'

'No. I was told on the phone it was the top floor. I've been looking for a garden flat,' she said, nodding in the direction of the boy, 'but I've found nothing I can afford.'

'Watch your kid on the road,' I said. 'It's full of learner drivers. It's on one of the routes, you see.'

'Aren't they the careful ones?' she said cockily.

She and the boy waited for my reply.

'You have a point,' I said, and let myself in. 'I'd like to show you around, but . . .'

'Yes, yes,' she said wearily, and waved me in.

'It's close to the park,' I said, sounding vaguely apologetic.

'Yes,' she said, 'that's something.'

The weather had been changeable, but just then there was a large patch of blue sky and a warm breeze in my face. I walked down the street towards my car with my jacket slung over my shoulder.

'Harry,' said the voice in a pleasant, easy tone. 'Mr Clements wants a word with you.'

Now, who was Mr Clements? Did he fill the shoes of my former boss, Mr Hamilton? Yes. I was sure he did.

I turned. I gave the young man my best blank stare. He was a chap. There was no doubt. His smile matched the pleasant, easy tone of his voice. A nasty bit of work. Revelled in the tough-boy training at Gosport. I could see it in his face. Came top of his class. I could see his halo. It resembled the circle of luminous dots on my wind-up alarm clock. I gathered from the way he was standing that he led with the left boot or fist.

'We've been watching you, Harry-boy . . .' he said.

Harry-boy – I had ten years on him.

He spoke into the roof of his mouth as if it might make him taller. He rolled his words to make them sound posh.

'We know all about your capers, don't we?'

Don't we – I intensely disliked the way these monkeys invoked the royal we.

I didn't attempt to sidestep him. I wanted to preserve the measure of distance between us.

'This way, Harry,' he said, holding out a helpful hand to indicate that I should turn and walk ahead of him. I was sure there were others. Two, I speculated, but I couldn't see them.

George may have known something about what he termed 'my capers' but he didn't know about the lump of metal that was swinging gently in the pocket of my jacket. He was still smiling and I had a decision to make.